"I have to disappe

Amanda's heart pounded in anticipation even as she uttered the halfhearted resistance.

"I always wondered," Blake whispered, "if you really tasted as good as I remembered." He rubbed his thumb on her lower lip. "May I?"

She didn't think, just nodded her head.

With a deep groan, he took her lips with a force that made Amanda whimper. No one had ever kissed her as if he was too hungry to let her go.

He wrapped her in his arms, and when he pressed her lips open, she gladly let him in. She pressed closer to Blake, her breasts crushing against his broad chest.

Heat sprang between them, and her body sizzled with want. Low in her belly, the recognition of her yearning for this man kindled something she hadn't felt in too long.

Amanda rubbed her hands over the strength of his muscles, the broadness of his shoulders, the narrowness at his waist. His response to her touch was primal and immediate. Blake wanted her. As much as she wanted him....

"Blake, I can't stay,"

ROBIN PERINI

COWBOY IN THE CROSSFIRE

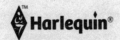
™ **Harlequin**®

TORONTO NEW YORK LONDON
AMSTERDAM PARIS SYDNEY HAMBURG
STOCKHOLM ATHENS TOKYO MILAN MADRID
PRAGUE WARSAW BUDAPEST AUCKLAND

For my dad—my hero. His love for our family inspires me.
He taught me that a man can be tough and tender, strong and
loyal, wise and funny—and he taught me to shoot and dragged
me all over West Texas on adventures, which came in mighty
handy while writing this book!
I love you, Dad. Always!

ISBN-13: 978-0-373-69629-1

COWBOY IN THE CROSSFIRE

Copyright © 2012 by Robin L. Perini

ABOUT THE AUTHOR

Award-winning author Robin Perini's love of heart stopping suspense and poignant romance, coupled with her adoration of high-tech weaponry and covert ops, encouraged her secret inner commando to take on the challenge of writing romantic suspense novels. Her mission's motto: "When danger and romance collide, no heart is safe."

Devoted to giving her readers fast-paced, high-stakes adventures with a love story sure to melt their hearts, Robin won the prestigious Romance Writers of America Golden Heart Award in 2011. By day she works for an advanced technology corporation, and in her spare time you might find her giving one of her many nationally acclaimed writing workshops or training in competitive small-bore rifle silhouette shooting. Robin loves to interact with readers. You can catch her on her website, www.robinperini.com, several major social-networking sites or write to her at P.O. Box 50472, Albuquerque, NM 87181-0472.

Books by Robin Perini

HARLEQUIN INTRIGUE
1340—FINDING HER SON
1362—COWBOY IN THE CROSSFIRE

CAST OF CHARACTERS

Amanda Hawthorne—Determined to protect her son from a murderer, and out of options, she must seek help from the disgraced cop who her brother framed.

Blake Redmond—This by-the-book sheriff never crosses the line. Can he ignore his badge to protect a fugitive and her son from those willing to kill anyone who gets in their way?

Ethan Hawthorne—Amanda's son can identify his uncle's killer. Now the five-year-old witness is the next target.

Logan Carmichael—Blake trusts the private investigator with his and Amanda's lives, but will Logan stay loyal when powerful forces threaten to take away everything he holds dear?

Vince Hawthorne—His secrets got him killed. Can Blake and Amanda find the evidence Vince left behind in time to save Ethan's life?

Shaun O'Connor—Why does the Internal Affairs cop offer to help? Is he out for justice or is he involved in murder?

Paul Irving—The lieutenant tried to save Blake's job. Is Paul now a target?

Matt Johnson—The detective got in over his head. Can he find a way out?

Rafe Vargas—The former special ops soldier knows how to kill. Can his loyalty be bought?

Deputy Parris—Blake's right-hand man was in line to be sheriff until Blake returned to Carder, Texas. Does Parris want the job at any cost?

Chapter One

A wicked gust of winter wind buffeted Amanda Hawthorne toward the front entrance of her brother's home. She wrapped her flimsy coat tighter around her body and lowered her head. Another cold blast nearly knocked her down. Even the weather fought to keep her out of Vince's house. Well, this freak ice storm wouldn't win, and neither would her brother. He'd be furious, but she was staying. Just until she found another job.

She breathed in, hoping to kill the perpetual French-fry smell that permeated her clothes from her final shift at Jimmy's Chicken Shack. She could have lived with the odor and her aching feet, but she couldn't take his octopus hands, his foul breath or his large body trapping her against the wall in his storage room. She shuddered at the memory. She wouldn't go back. But first, she had to face Vince.

With a deep breath, she unlocked the door. "Big brother, I've got bad news. You may have houseguests for a while—"

Her voice trailed off. The photos that had lined the entryway hall lay shattered on the tile floor. The small table near the doorway teetered on its side, crushed.

"Vince?" Her heart thumped like a panicked rabbit.

She ran into the living room. The place was in shambles. "Ethan?" Oh, God. Where was her son?

She rounded the couch and skidded to a halt. Vince lay on the floor in a pool of blood, eyes staring up at her, sightless. A hole in his chest, a gun in his hand.

Her knees shook and she swayed. *No.*

She whirled around the room, frantic, searching. "Ethan!" she screamed. He had to be here. He had to be okay. He was only five. "Ethan, where are you?"

Deadly silence echoed through the house. Her body went numb. This couldn't be happening. Her son was her life.

Then she saw it. A small, bloody footprint on the wood floor. Streaks of red trailed across the carpet toward the entertainment center. So much blood. Too much blood.

"No!"

A horrified, wounded cry ricocheted through the quiet room.

The sound came from her.

Shaking, her mind whirling through unthinkable images, she followed the blood to the cabinet. Sobs clutched her throat as she tossed aside a slew of DVDs dumped in front of the oak furniture. Bracing herself for the worst, she held her breath and opened the door.

Empty.

She clutched at the wood to keep herself from collapsing. "Ethan!" Her stomach roiled. She should never have left him. Ever!

A choked whimper broke from behind another section on the unit.

"Ethan?"

She snatched the brass handle and yanked it open

to reveal her five-year-old huddled in a ball, rocking back and forth.

Alive.

Amanda's knees quaked with relief. She couldn't stop the tears that poured down her face. Her son was alive. She snatched him from the cabinet and folded him into her arms. She couldn't stop touching him. His arms, his legs, his hair, his tear-streaked face. With a trembling hand, she stroked his blood-stained pants. "Are you hurt?"

He shook his head. "U-Uncle Vince."

"I know, little man. I know." She rocked him back and forth, her chin on his soft hair. His small arms clung to her as if he would never let her go. "It's okay. Mommy's here." She repeated the words over and over again, as much for herself as for Ethan.

She shot up a thankful prayer, then her gaze fell to her brother's body. Blindly, Amanda searched for the cell in her pocket to call 9-1-1. She pulled out the phone and started dialing.

Ethan grabbed her hand, his eyes wild with panic. "No, Mommy. Uncle Vince said for us to run away."

She clasped Ethan to her, trying to calm him even as an icy wave of terror threatened to freeze her from the inside. Vince had been a stand-and-fight kind of guy. A cop. If he'd said that, then they weren't safe in this house. Maybe not safe anywhere.

"Where?" she murmured. "Where can we go?"

Ethan wrapped his arms tight and squeezed. "Blake. Go to Blake," he whispered in her ear, his voice shaking with a terror no child should ever feel.

She stilled. "Where did you hear that name, little man?"

"Uncle Vince." Ethan buried his face in the crook of her neck. "Go to Blake."

Ethan stuck his thumb in his mouth, something he hadn't done in over a year.

Go to Blake? Why would Vince say such a thing? Blake Redmond hated her brother. No way was she going to Blake for anything. She'd take care of herself and her son.

Pressing Ethan's face against her shoulder, she ran to her brother's body. With a gulp, she crouched down. She snatched the gun from Vince's hand for protection, hurried to his desk and wrenched open the drawer. Thank goodness. The grocery money was still in the bank bag. She stuffed it and the gun into her purse.

Amanda carried Ethan to the front hallway, pried her son's arms from around her and set him down. "We're getting out of here, Ethan." She kissed his forehead, then bundled him into his navy-and-orange coat, scarf and gloves. She tugged on his hat and covered his ears.

Ethan sneaked a look into the living room at Vince, and his face went blank. He'd shut down. Amanda gave his hat a last tug. "Don't worry, Mommy will take care of you."

With Ethan in her arms, she raced out of Vince's house into the cold late-November night. How would she ever make things all right? She had nowhere to go, no one to help her. She only knew they had to get away.

Hands shaking, she unlocked the car, tossed her purse inside and settled Ethan into his booster seat. He scooted back. She brushed his hair aside. "We'll be safe."

Someone grabbed her from behind. "You won't keep the promise," the deep voice sounded in her ear.

Amanda whirled around. A man in a ski mask loomed above her. She shot a panicked glance to the car. The gun was still in her purse. She reached into her pocket for her phone. The man grabbed the cell, threw it to the ground and rammed her against the car. "Where did Vince hide it?"

"What are you—"

"No games." His grip tightened. "Tell me, and you and the kid live."

The cold look in his eyes belied his words. He'd never let them go.

"Where's Vince's file?"

The man's arm pinned her neck. He pressed against her windpipe, harder and harder. She gasped for air, tried to pry him away. Stars exploded in front of her. Blackness threatened to swallow her whole. Oh, God. She was dying.

"Mommy!"

At Ethan's scream, the man's hold slackened. Just enough.

"No!" she choked. Aiming for his knee, Amanda kicked out hard. She heard a sickening pop. With a shout, he fell to the ground, clutching his leg.

She dived into the front seat, shoved the key into the ignition and jammed the car into gear. The attacker struggled to his feet, cursing at her.

Amanda backed through Vince's front yard and spun into the street.

Shots rang out, followed by the thwack of bullets hitting metal. Fire seared across her side. Half-crazy with shock and fear, she punched the accelerator. Her car jerked forward and sped down the street, but not before she saw the man limp to his car and start after them.

He would not get Ethan. She'd die first.

In desperation, she screeched around a turn into an

alley. Headlights followed dizzyingly in her rearview mirror. She had to lose him. "Are you all right, Ethan?"

His panicked whimper was the only sound from the backseat. Oh, no. Had he been hit? She twisted around to check on him even as pain sliced across her ribs. Fighting through the agony, she scanned her son. He was in shock but looked unhurt. Unlike herself. Amanda pressed her palm hard against her side. It was warm and wet.

She stared at her hand. It was red. Very, very red.

She'd been shot.

Right through the door.

Her panting matched Ethan's. Her fingers had gone numb with cold. She had to stop the bleeding or she'd pass out. She gripped the steering wheel tight. Think, Amanda. Think of someplace safe to stop.

A quick right, then left brought her to a dark side street. She floored it and streaked toward Main. With a quick prayer, she skidded to a halt in a parking lot full of cars and turned off the engine and lights.

"Duck, Ethan. Hide."

He slid out of the booster seat and sank to the floorboard. Trying to ignore the pulsing pain in her side, Amanda crouched low against the cracked vinyl. With one hand she reached back and stroked Ethan's head, buried in his arms. She tried to comfort him without words, but his body trembled, and her heart ached.

With the other hand, she searched her purse for the gun. Holding the weapon firmly, she shrank down even more and gripped the butt hard. Her fingers shook. *Please, let her live. Let her keep Ethan safe.*

The cold seeped into her skin. Every shallow breath turned into a visible wisp of air.

"Mommy? I'm scared."

Ethan's small voice pierced her heart. "We're okay, little man." She kept her voice calm and reassuring, while inside the panic had her heart galloping. "We just have to be very, very quiet."

"So the bad man doesn't find us?"

"Yes, sweetie. Hush now."

His sniffles were the only sound as she waited. Headlights passed by, but she couldn't chance raising her head. Her fingers cramped around the metal of the gun. She stayed still. Seconds dragged into minutes as she waited, praying no one would see or hear anything.

After what seemed an eternity, Amanda sagged against the seat. "I think it's safe."

At her words, Ethan scrambled into the front and dived into her arms, his face streaked with tears. She fought not to cry out in pain, but couldn't stop a small gasp.

He leaped back. "Are you hurt? Like Uncle Vince?"

"I'm fine, honey. Just fine."

But she wasn't. And she knew it. She grabbed her thin scarf and used one end to pad her wound, the other she wrapped around her torso. The makeshift bandage would have to do. She had bigger problems. The gunman knew her. He'd seen Ethan. The bullet-ridden car would be easy to spot, and she couldn't risk being found.

Vince had warned her if anything bad happened to him not to stay in Austin. No matter what. She had to get out. Amanda scanned the parking lot. Her ex's penchant for stealing cars would come in handy. She could use the lock jimmy Ethan's father had left under the seat to break in to and hot-wire a car.

She clutched the handle, but the simple movement nearly tore her insides. She bit her lip. If anything happened to her... She stared at Ethan, his lips trembling, his expression haunted. They needed help.

Gritting her teeth, she slipped out of the car and into the night. She had no choice. She had to go to Blake.

SHERIFF BLAKE REDMOND paced the wooden floor, nerves wound tighter than an overcinched saddle. He had a bad feeling about tonight but didn't know why. Sleet pounded the roof, hammering the century-old ranch house with what the Weather Channel had termed the worst ice storm in decades. Four-foot-long icicles and West Texas didn't go together.

Below-freezing temperatures and unrelenting ice made travel deadly. He'd issued an order hours ago for folks in his county to hunker down until further notice, but there were always those fools who didn't listen.

A whine escaped the Lab mix curled on the rug next to the fire.

"I know, boy." Blake glanced at the old police radio sitting silent on the hand-carved sofa table. He'd spent several hours tinkering with the ancient equipment. A few paper clips and pencil erasers strategically placed, and it worked like a new one. "Gonna be a long night, Leo."

The dog rose and paced the floor, unable to settle.

"You feel it, too?"

Blake bent and ruffled the oddly shaped ears of the stray mutt. He'd wandered into his barn shortly after Blake had moved back to Carder, Texas, to take over as sheriff following his father's sudden death. The dog had hung around until finally they'd both surrendered to the inevitable.

The animal's unease didn't bode well, and the sparse living room gave Blake no distraction. Despite moving into his childhood ranch home nine months ago, Blake still kept his memories stored away in boxes. Easier to avoid them that way.

The police radio cracked with static, and the dispatcher's voice broke through the old speaker. "Sheriff?"

Blake snagged the microphone. "Donna, are you still manning the station? I ordered you home hours ago."

"Deputy Parris just called in. Streets are clear, though he couldn't stop complaining the storm ruined his trip to his fishing cabin."

"No one's supposed to be on these roads tonight but me. If Mom finds out her best friend's working on a night like this, I'm dead. Go home."

"You're like your father," Donna said.

Which meant she ignored Blake's orders, too. Maybe that's where his unease had originated. Donna had run the Sheriff's Office dispatch for his father since he was a kid. He'd inherited her just like he had the job. He'd also learned from his dad exactly how to handle her. "Go home, Donna. Or I'll put you in jail and lock away the key to be sure you're safe."

"Yep, just like him." She chuckled. "Dispatch out."

Blake glanced at the clock. He'd give her fifteen minutes. On his patrol, he'd verify she got home. He tugged on a wool sweater over his corduroys. His uniform didn't have the warmth he'd need tonight.

A low growl rumbled from Leo. The dog rose and his ears lay back as he stared at the front door. Blake tensed, his hand automatically going to his sidearm. A movement outside the front window caught Blake's attention. A pair of blue eyes under a thatch of reddish-brown hair peered just above the windowsill. Right at him.

"What the hell…"

Blake flung open the door. Freezing wind and

needles of sleet invaded the room. A small boy huddled in a Chicago Bears coat and scarf stared up at him, his cheeks red, his lips blue, dried blood on his pants. "My mommy's dying. She said you'd help us."

The boy sank to his knees.

With an inward curse, Blake scooped up the shaking child, kicked the door shut and sat him down by the fire. He crouched down and slid the boy's pant leg up to his knee. No obvious injury. "Where did this blood come from, son? Are you hurt?"

The boy shook his head and pursed his lips together. "Please. Help Mommy."

"Where is she?"

"Our car slid. It crashed." The boy's eyes filled with tears. "Mommy kept falling asleep. She made me leave her."

No one could survive for long in that storm. Blake shoved his arms into his shearling coat, yanked on his gloves and grabbed a flashlight from the top of the refrigerator. "Is it only your mom out there? No one else?"

The boy nodded. "Only Mommy."

"Stay here. Understand?" The kid couldn't have walked far. His mother had to be nearby. "Leo, come."

The dog, who'd been nosing at their small visitor, bounded to Blake. The boy waited pathetically in front of the fire, shivering, yet his eyes locked on Blake. "Are you a good guy?"

Blake pulled his Stetson down over his ears. "You can trust me."

The boy's lips quivered in uncertainty. He was a brave little guy. A sharp pang twisted Blake's heart. Did every boy practice that same look? In that one instant, he'd looked…just like Joey. Just like the son Blake had lost.

He shoved the pain into the hole where his heart had been. "I'll be right back. Stay by the fire. Don't touch anything." He gave the kid his most stern look.

With Leo at his side, Blake yanked open the door and stepped into the frozen night. The lights from the barn were bare flickers against the onslaught of sleet and roaring wind. Ice pricked his face, making his eyes water. He scanned for any movement through the darkness. Nothing between here and the horse barn. He had only minutes or the boy's mother was dead.

Long icicles dangled from the porch eaves and looked like something out of a horror movie. He shoved through them, breaking off several. They fell to the steps, the howl of the winter wind swallowing all sound.

Even if the woman were screaming he wouldn't hear her until he tripped over her body. He swept his flashlight across shiny layers of ice. As he stepped past a large pine, blinking orange just at the edge of his vision caught his attention. Hazard lights. Tilted. The car must be in the ditch. He veered toward the vehicle, but Leo barked, tugged on Blake's sleeve and shot in the opposite direction.

"You'd better be right, mutt." Blake hurried after the animal, swinging his light toward a small gully that lined his long driveway.

Nothing was visible from the road. When he reached the edge and shined the beam into the ditch, Leo leaped toward a small, snow-covered figure, huddled out of sight of the driveway. Blake slid down the frozen dirt and turned her over. If it hadn't been for her son and the dog, Blake may never have found her in this mess. She was soaked and freezing, but a small puff of air escaped her nose. Thank God.

He lifted her into his arms, and she moaned, squirming, pushing at him. "Ethan—"

"Your boy's fine," Blake said. "Now stay still or we'll both freeze to death."

"Blake?" She clutched at his collar feebly. "Please. Help us."

Blake's ears had gone numb, but he could have sworn she said his name, although with this wind he couldn't be sure. He could barely feel his hands, even through the gloves. She must be closing in on hypothermia. He had to get her inside. Fast.

He struggled up the gully, his boots losing traction even though she didn't weigh more than a minute. Each step was treacherous. Leo raced past Blake to the porch light as he slugged his way home. The wind and sleet slammed at him from the side. He stumbled, jostling her to maintain his balance. She whimpered in his arms.

Blake's legs stung with cold. Each step took more and more effort. He squinted toward his house. The curtain pushed back, and a small face pressed to the front window. The ranch house looked unbelievably far away. By the time he reached the porch, the woman in his arms quivered uncontrollably.

The boy flung open the door, his face streaked with tears. "Mommy? Is she…dead?"

Blake shouldered past the kid and laid his mother on the sofa. What kind of youngster asked a question like that? Ignoring his own tingling hands and feet, he shrugged out of his coat, tossed it and his Stetson on the chair, and knelt beside the unconscious woman. "Is your name Ethan?"

Wide-eyed, the boy nodded.

"How old are you?"

He held up five fingers, and Blake nodded. "I thought so. What's your mom's name?"

"Mommy."

Not much help there. Blake pulled the scarf and hat from the woman's face. A tumble of wild, auburn curls fell to her shoulders. He rocked back on his heels in shocked recognition.

Amanda.

He couldn't believe it was her. The woman he'd nearly lost his senses to beneath the mistletoe one very memorable Christmas Eve. The woman who'd tempted him beyond endurance. The woman he'd known he could never have because she was his best friend's sister. And she'd almost died.

"Amanda?" What was that bastard Vince's sister doing in the middle of an ice storm four-hundred miles from home?

Ethan scooted under Blake's arm and laid a small hand on his mother's cheek. "Mommy?" he whispered. "Wake up. Please. I'm scared."

At the boy's plaintive words, Blake nearly doubled over. Had his four-year-old son said the same thing to his mother after the accident? Blake knew from the autopsy report his ex-wife had died instantly, but Joey had lived for several minutes after their car had been blindsided. His son had been alone, frightened and dying, probably begging for his mother to wake up. Maybe calling for his father to save him. But Blake hadn't been there.

Well, he was here now. For Amanda. He ripped off her gloves and clasped her hands. Ice-cold. No way could he warm her in these wet clothes. He unzipped her insubstantial coat. The right side of her shirt was soaked in blood.

"What the hell?"

He pushed the denim aside and stared at the injury just below and outside the soft curve of her left breast. He recognized a gunshot wound when he saw one.

Blake grabbed a clean dish towel from the kitchen and pressed it to the gash, causing Amanda to moan. "Get your coat on, kid. We're taking your mom to the doctor." One look out the window told him the ride would be an interesting trip. The visibility had deteriorated even more in the last few minutes. "Hopefully I'll get us to the hospital in one piece."

Amanda stirred restlessly on the couch.

He nabbed the microphone from the sofa table. "Parris, this is Blake." The static from the line shattered the night. "Deputy, you there?"

Amanda tugged at his arm with a weak but desperate grip. "No hospital," she whispered. "Hide us. Please. Or we're dead."

The stark words ricocheted through Blake as she struggled to sit, then collapsed in his arms. He eased her down, and pushed back the curls surrounding her face. She was hurt, and vulnerable, and she couldn't tell him why. What had she gotten herself into that she'd risk her life to stay hidden?

He glanced at Ethan. With the gunshot wound, Blake had to give her the benefit of the doubt. If she was telling the truth, he refused to put the boy's life in jeopardy.

"Sheriff? You heading out on patrol?" The ghost of a voice broke through the crackling radio.

"Not yet. Parris, let me know if you or Smithson see any strangers wandering the town. I'll get back to you."

He knelt next to the sofa and studied his unexpected visitor. Amanda had changed in the last six months. Thinner, her skin nearly translucent. Circles beneath her eyes, but still so beautiful, he had to remind himself to breathe. She'd obviously been through hell. Blake motioned to the boy whose eyes had grown wide and fear-filled. "Ethan? How did your mom get hurt?"

The boy looked at his unconscious mother and shook his head. "I promised I wouldn't tell."

Secrets. They burned Blake's gut. He'd experienced too many in Austin. At the same time, he admired Amanda's kid. Blake recognized Ethan's terror from his trembling hands. The boy wanted to cry but bit down on his lip, fighting against the panic. Amanda's son showed more courage in that moment than most grown men Blake had witnessed facing a gun on the streets.

He crouched so he was eye to eye with the boy. "Promises are important, but your mom came to me for help. I'm one of the good guys, remember?"

Ethan simply stared at Blake, his eyes too suspicious for a boy of five. "Mommy?" His tentative hand tugged at his mother's sleeve.

"She's hurt, Ethan. But she doesn't want to go to the doctor. I need to know what happened. I want to make her well."

The boy shifted back and forth, stared at his unconscious mother, then back at Blake. He lifted his chin and met Blake's gaze. "A bad man tried to hurt us. Mommy saved me."

THE BED WAS SOFT, the room dark except for a small nightlight. Amanda felt warm for the first time in hours. She must be dead. There didn't seem to be any other explanation.

She shifted. Her flesh burned like fire. This definitely wasn't heaven.

Reality came flooding back.

Vince. Ethan.

She tried to sit up, but a sharp, blazing pain pierced her side. She fell back with a groan.

"Not a good move, considering you tried to stop a bullet with your body."

She'd recognize the soft drawl of that voice anywhere.

Blake Redmond.

She scanned up from his worn cowboy boots, past his corduroys to a dark green sweater that emphasized the flecks of jade and gold in his glittering eyes. She'd expected the typical tan sheriff's uniform at least. Still, she could see he was no longer a big-city Austin cop. All he needed was a cowboy hat to complete the picture of a small-town lawman. Not a friendly one, though.

Even with the dim light she could tell his face was carved in stone. Her heart skipped a beat. What had he found out? Had he called the deputy? Even now, was the man who murdered Vince and tried to kill her on his way here? Guarding her ribs, she struggled to swing her legs over the bed's edge.

Blake rushed over and pressed her back against the pillow. "Don't even think about getting out of this bed. Not until I look at that wound."

"Where's Ethan? Is he safe?"

Blake placed a medical kit on the nightstand and flipped on a small bedside light. "Hunkered down with my crazy mutt glued to his side. First door on the right. They're fine. I won't say the same for you."

"Did you tell your deputy about us?" she countered.

"Trying to sidestep the issue?" Blake opened the supplies. "You can thank your boy I didn't ignore your request. I didn't like his responses to my questions." Blake sat on the bed next to her and unpacked bandages, hydrogen peroxide and antibiotic ointment. "That doesn't mean I don't want answers from you."

"What did Ethan say?"

Blake's jaw tightened with irritation. "Not much. His mother's been shot and has passed out. He's dependent on a man he's never met." He glared at her. "He's scared."

The stark statement shattered a piece of Amanda's heart.

Blake dragged a chair next to the bed. "What's going on?"

She studied him warily. She didn't know what to say. Blake prided himself on being honest. A by-the-book kind of guy. She doubted he'd appreciate what she'd been forced to do over the last day.

Not that she regretted one action. To keep her son safe, Amanda would do *anything*.

Anything.

And her horrifying suspicions? The unspeakable theory she'd pieced together on that long drive from snippets of a few conversations and emails with Vince over the past few months. Should she tell Blake what she suspected about the death of his ex-wife and child? She had no proof. What if she was wrong? Why hurt him more? Better to remain silent.

Blake waited, then shook his head. "Fine. Don't imagine I won't figure it out." He stood and opened the first aid box. "Unfasten your shirt and lay on your side," he said, his voice gruff. "This is gonna hurt."

No kidding. She unbuttoned the bottom half of the shirt and rolled to her right. He pushed the denim out of the way, his fingers gentle. Somehow, when she'd fantasized about him touching her bare skin, it had never involved a bullet wound. She stared at his lean hips and focused hard, trying to distract herself with inappropri-ately lascivious thoughts. Anything rather than cry and act like a wimp in front of him.

He unscrewed a bottle of antiseptic. She ventured a glance at him. He hadn't changed much. He still wore his light brown hair short, although it was long enough to run her fingers through. His hazel eyes flickered in the light, and she could have sworn flecks of gold glittered as he glanced down at her. He was one of the sexiest men she'd ever met. And so wrong for her. His wife had just left him when she'd met him in Austin, so she'd ignored the flip-flop of her belly whenever he'd entered the room. Until that one Christmas Eve after his divorce finalized, that one amazing kiss. She had no business thinking about Blake in that way. She had to focus on her and Ethan's safety, but just for the next few minutes, maybe…

She shivered as he bared more of her torso. He probed at the sensitive skin she couldn't quite see. She sucked in a sharp breath. Okay, so much for the distraction-from-pain theory.

That hurt.

"When did you get shot?" he muttered.

The agonizingly long trip flashed through her mind. Town after town. Dairy Queen after Dairy Queen. Ethan being as patient as a five-year-old could, as if he under-stood she only had small reserves left. "I don't know. Sixteen, eighteen hours. Forever. The storm slowed us to a crawl. Five miles an hour some stretches."

"You should have stopped."

He pressed against the fevered skin, and slowly, pain-fully worked the dried, blood-soaked scarf away from the wound. She winced at each tug, tears stinging her eyes. She wanted to scream. She held her breath until finally he pulled away the last of the material.

She sagged in relief.

"Luckily the bullet didn't lodge inside. Bad news is the wound is inflamed. I've got ointment, Amanda, but you need a doctor. And antibiotics."

"Doctors report gunshot wounds."

"So do sheriffs." He explored the area one last time, then sucked in a slow breath. "Brace yourself."

The cold sting of peroxide hissed on her skin. She clutched at the sheets and bit down on her lip to keep from crying out. She didn't know how close Ethan was. She couldn't let him see her like this. He'd been through enough.

Blake quickly rubbed on antibiotic ointment, then covered the wound with a pad. "I need to secure the dressing. Sit up for me."

He supported her back as she rose. When she was steady, he unfastened the remainder of the buttons on her shirt. Her cheeks burned. She hadn't been able to wear a bra since it happened, and there was no getting around him touching her as he quickly wrapped the bandage around her torso.

Finally, he secured a last piece of tape. With jerky movements he rose from the bed and grabbed a large Dallas Cowboys sweatshirt from the drawer. "You can wear this. Your son doesn't need to see all that blood."

Hovering over her, Blake eased the soiled material off with the prowess of a cowboy who'd undressed his share of women. His touch lingered on her naked back before he choked out a cough and slipped on the clean, dry sweatshirt.

The awareness between them sizzled. She chanced a look over her shoulder. She'd never seen Blake more uncomfortable as he eased away from the bed. He planted himself in the center of the bedroom and crossed his arms, piercing her with a glare she welcomed. If he'd smiled or given her a soft, sexy grin, she might have done something stupid.

"Thank you." She lifted her gaze and saw his cheeks flush before he turned on her.

"We're not finished yet." He stiffened his back. "I have some antibiotics in the barn. I'll be right back."

She heard the door open, and the harsh whistling of wind sounded from the other room before the oak slammed closed. He was going out into this monster storm. For her.

Who did that?

No one she knew, that's for sure.

She rubbed her eyes. She had to think clearly. She was a fugitive, but Blake didn't need to know that. She just had to keep her wits about her, get well and move on. Don't let herself be taken in by a man who was like a hero out of a fairy tale. One step at a time, and she could put some miles between her and Blake. A lot of miles if she had her way.

She twisted, testing the bandage, trying once again to sit up.

"You're gonna undo all my handiwork."

Blake strode into the room, holding a prescription bottle and a glass of water. "The antibiotics were for the foal, but it's better than nothing. Should be the right dose."

"You want to feed me horse pills? Are you crazy?"

"You wanted my help. It's this or a doctor. You've got a fever."

She studied his face and could see he was deadly serious. Showing herself at any medical facility would put a target on her and Ethan. She had to stay under the radar for as long as she could. *She* wasn't the criminal.

Well, not exactly. And certainly not voluntarily.

She snagged the pill and swallowed it with a grimace.

Blake studied her, his expression unwavering and speculative. "Just how much trouble are you in, Amanda? You take a horse pill to avoid the hospital, you drive eighteen hours in an ice storm after a bullet cut a furrow in your side. What are you doing here? Is your brother going to knock on my door next?"

So much for the fairy tale. She lifted her chin and swiped at her hair. "Vince is dead."

The muscle of his jaw throbbed briefly. The only sign he cared at all.

"Aren't you going to say anything? He was your best friend."

"Best friend?" Blake crossed his arms, his expression grim. "Really? Is that what he was when he sold me out? When he didn't show up for my son's funeral?"

"He didn't think you'd want him there."

"He was right."

Amanda rubbed her hands over her eyes to keep from looking into his perceptive gaze. He'd recognize the guilt, the secret knowledge. "There was never any proof Vince gave Internal Affairs evidence against you."

"Only one person could've set me up to take the fall. Vince. You can lie to yourself, but don't lie to me. I've had enough of that to last a lifetime." Blake leaned over the bed, crowding her. She shrank back against the sheets.

"Don't hurt my mommy!"

Ethan launched across the room, the dog racing after him. The boy grabbed Blake around the legs and started pounding at him. The sight of her usually gentle son taking all his anger and fear out on Blake savaged Amanda's soul. Would he ever be the same after what he'd seen? She shoved off the bed as Blake stopped and calmly grasped Ethan's arms.

"I don't hurt people, son. I'm a policeman."

Ethan wrenched away. "Policemen are bad. Police made Uncle Vince dead."

Chapter Two

Cops killed Vince?

Blake dropped his hands, and Ethan dived into his mother's arms. Amanda winced but hugged him close, murmuring words of comfort. Her wound had to be hurting like the devil, but she simply stroked Ethan's head, rocking him to and fro. The only sign of pain was the tightness around her mouth and the color draining from her face. Incredible. The love that shone there twisted something inside Blake, touched some hidden place that needed to stay protected.

"It's okay, little man," she whispered. "I'll keep us safe. I promise."

She had more courage than Vince ever did. Blake had tried to convince his friend to work together to investigate and take down the dirty cops. Vince had done the opposite. He'd jumped in headfirst with the enemy, then helped set up Blake to take the fall for missing evidence and confiscated money from several drug busts.

Ethan's sobs turned to hiccups. Blake's jaw ached as he tried to contain his fury. Vince's cowardice had dragged that innocent boy into God knows what.

Ethan, nestled against Amanda's chest and clearly exhausted, fell asleep in only a few minutes. She kissed the top of his head and tried to stand. She trembled and swayed.

Blake wanted to punch his fist through the wall. He'd traumatized the boy even more. His stomach churned at the thought, acid hitting the back of his throat. He gulped down the guilt and reached out to steady her with a gentle touch. "I'll take Ethan."

Her hold tightened. She didn't trust anyone else with him. He got that, but he also knew her legs quivered underneath her. She was near collapse. He stilled, waiting patiently, his arms open. Finally, as if her energy left her, she nodded. Blake lifted the sleeping boy. The actions, the familiar, precious weight of his little body poked at the empty ache inside of Blake. The boy snuggled closer, and Blake's throat closed off at the swell of emotions. Ethan was vulnerable and trusting enough in sleep to let a stranger hold him. A child's faith.

The dog at his heels, Blake carried Amanda's son down the hall and tucked him beneath the covers. His gaze lingered on Ethan's tear-stained cheeks. Blake knotted his hands into fists. No child deserved to face this kind of fear. He hated that Ethan feared law enforcement—the people he should trust.

Leo whined and Blake gave the dog a nod. The mutt jumped onto the bed and settled next to Ethan. The boy would be okay, but Blake needed answers from Amanda. She was keeping secrets. He couldn't allow that. Ethan wasn't going to feel unsafe. Not on Blake's watch.

He stalked out of the room and grabbed the door, ready to slam it, then stopped himself. Softly, he eased it shut, strode through the doorway and closed him and Amanda into the guest bedroom. "No more games. Is what Ethan said true?"

"Why do you think I never went to a hospital? Vince was murdered. By a cop."

"I figured that one out."

As many times as Blake had cursed his former best friend for being a low-down, belly-crawling coward, he hadn't wanted him dead. Nailed for bribery. Definitely. Confessing to the police area commander how Vince had framed Blake. Most assuredly.

But not dead.

Blake crossed his arms and ignored the fatigue and vulnerability in her eyes. He wouldn't let himself get sucked in. He had to protect Ethan. "Who did it?"

"I don't know." Amanda shifted her focus toward the door. "I should go to him."

Her gaze flickered left, and she twirled a strand of her curly hair. Vince had joked about the obvious tell. He'd warned Blake if he ever played poker with Amanda, twisting her hair was a sure sign of a bluff.

"Your brother lied to me every damn day the last six months I was in Austin. I've learned how to spot deceit, so don't bother trying it." Her pretty mouth opened slightly in surprise, and he let out a harsh laugh. "Yeah, I can see your wheels turning. I may be a small-town sheriff now, but I've still got big-city instincts."

"I'm not lying."

He eased toward her. "Fine. Keep your secrets. As soon as this storm ends, you can fight your own battles." He paused. "Without Ethan in the middle of them. He'll stay with me."

"You have no right—"

"I do if I think your son's in danger." He leaned back against the dressing table. "Did you get in the middle of one of Vince's dirty deals? Is that how you got shot?"

"Take that back." She jumped to her feet, then doubled over with a whimper. Her knees buckled, and she sagged to the floor.

Blake cursed and reached for her. He'd have thought she was feigning pain to distract him except her face had turned a scary shade of gray. He didn't want to hurt her. He wanted her to tell him the truth. To give him the information he needed to protect them both. No matter what trouble she'd gotten into, she didn't deserve this. Neither did Ethan.

"Don't touch me." She scooted away from him.

"Shut up. You're hurt, and you've lost a lot of blood. Get up too fast and you'll keel over every time."

He took one step, swept her into his arms and strode to the bed, pretending to ignore the blue-and-silver sweatshirt that slid down one shoulder and the bare skin of her legs against his arm. Gently, he laid her down and tucked a pillow behind her. He dragged a chair over and straddled it. "I can see you love Ethan, but you can't protect him."

"Thanks for the vote of confidence."

She was silent. Blake met her gaze, his own steady and resolute. He could see her wavering and leaned forward. "You came here for a reason, Amanda. Let me help you."

She rubbed her eyes with her hands and sighed in defeat. "Vince's last words were to Ethan. He said to come to you."

"That doesn't make sense. We haven't spoken since my father was killed and I left Austin. Why would he send you to me?"

"He always said you were the most honest cop he knew."

"He had a hell of a way of showing it." Blake stood and paced the bedroom floor.

"I didn't see the point in coming here. Maybe I was right. You hate Vince, but…" She shifted and her mouth twitched in pain, but she didn't complain, didn't say a word. "I was shot. If anything happened to me—" Her voice choked.

"Ethan would be alone," Blake finished. The fatigue, the fear, the pain had started to get to her. He could see it in her eyes. Blake sat on the side of the bed. "Then why won't you let me help?"

She pressed her hand to her side. "I'm alive. Tomorrow we'll leave, start a new life. It's the only way to be certain we're safe."

The crackling of the police radio in the other room made her jump. She clasped his arm. "Please, don't tell anyone we're here. I'm begging you. I'll do *anything*. Just don't give us away."

Blake removed her hand from his sweater. "Stay here," he muttered. He walked out of the room and down the hall, torn between duty and justice. Hell of it was, he understood. He would've done whatever it took to save Joey. Even his ex-wife, Kathy. He'd been called into the station for yet another Internal Affairs interview the afternoon of the accident. Kathy had picked up Joey from preschool instead of Blake. Maybe if he'd been in the car, with his reflexes, his training, he could have avoided the accident. Or at least made sure Joey survived… If Blake could have saved them, he would've sacrificed himself.

Slow but determined footsteps followed him down the hall. Not surprising. Amanda wouldn't leave anything to chance. Not when it came to her son. He got that.

He tried to ignore the fact she didn't trust him. The

truth chafed, but he didn't trust her, either. She knew more than she was telling. He could feel it.

"Sheriff?" His deputy's voice crackled through the living room. "Parris checking in."

Blake picked up the microphone. "Donna make it home?"

"Kicking and screaming." The older man chuckled. "Muttering about being on stand-by. She hasn't changed since your dad and I caught her staying all night at the station during that tornado warning fifteen years ago."

"Streets still clear? No one traveling in this mess?"

"Hank Stratton tried to make it to Charlie's Bar, but he slid down the driveway and crawled home. I told his wife to steal his boots. Should keep him from wandering outside. Other than that, the whole town's dead."

Blake slid a sidelong glance at Amanda, his pause longer than usual. "Could you check on my mom?"

There was silence on the radio. "You want *me* to check on her? You okay, Blake?"

"Keep your radio with you in case of emergencies."

"Are you serious? You're staying in?"

"I'm not patrolling tonight." Blake watched as Amanda teetered and swayed. She grabbed the table for support just as he wrapped his arm around her, careful to avoid her injury. Her slight frame leaned into him. He felt every curve pressing against him in a way he'd only imagined before now. His body tingled with awareness, his senses sharpened at her vulnerability. She needed him whether she knew it or not. "Keep me posted."

"Hell has officially frozen over. Parris out."

Blake set the radio down, and Amanda let out a relieved breath as he held her to his side, their closeness fanning the shimmering heat he couldn't deny. He gave her a sharp look. "Surprised I didn't have Parris run a check on you?"

"Frankly, yes."

"I don't lie, Amanda."

"Yeah, well, I've been burned more than once." She tried to straighten but winced, her left hand pressing against her bandage.

Amanda tugged away from him and planted her legs firmly. He could see she used every ounce of strength to stand and face him.

"Thank you for what you've done," she said. "When morning comes, we'll be out of your town and your life." She slowly turned, and with careful steps, walked into her bedroom, emerging a few seconds later with a pillow and small throw. She disappeared into Ethan's room without looking back.

At the soft click of the door, Blake sighed. He could still feel the imprint of her body against his. She might act brave, but she'd clung to him, and in doing so she'd ignited desire in his gut. A flame he'd thought had been doused for good. Apparently he'd been mistaken.

Pushing the tempting thoughts aside, Blake grabbed a cup of coffee and walked to his office. An internet search on Vince was definitely in order. Blake had been blinded by his anger toward his ex-partner, but he couldn't deny the truth of the current situation. Vince was dead. Amanda had been shot. Her son was at risk. Cops were involved, and not in a good way.

He wouldn't let her vanish with all those nonanswers she'd tried to pass off. He had his own unfinished business in Austin. If Vince had sent Amanda to him, there had to be a connection between the attack and his being drummed out of the Austin Police Department. Somewhere deep inside, he still wanted to believe he hadn't been completely wrong about Vince.

Blake booted the computer and typed his ex-partner's name into the search engine. He would discover the truth and protect Amanda and her son, whether she wanted his help or not.

AMANDA WOKE TO SUNLIGHT streaming through the slats in the room where Blake had bandaged her, not on the floor next to Ethan. She remembered shivering beside her son's bed, knowing she couldn't leave him alone except to throw his blood-soaked jeans in the washer. He'd hardly had any sleep since they left Austin. Each time she'd thought he'd rest for more than an hour, he'd jerked awake, screaming for Vince. Begging the bad cop to go away.

That's how she'd learned what really happened. That's why she'd veered from a trip to the hospital. She'd pressed her son to tell her more, but Ethan refused to say a word about what he'd seen. Except in his dreams.

And last night she hadn't been there for him.

She covered her eyes with her forearm. Blake must have moved her last night. But what about Ethan? She lay there for a few seconds, listening for his cries.

Not a sound.

She didn't like the quiet. Not one bit.

Amanda threw off the blankets piled on top of her and tried to sit up. Pain stabbed at her side. She groaned but didn't surrender to it. She could handle anything as long as she knew Ethan was safe. Holding her torso stiff, she opened her bedroom door and hurried into the next room, her bare feet cold on the hardwood floors.

Amanda nearly tripped over a rocking chair that hadn't been in the room last night. Ethan's clean jeans were folded neatly on the dresser. An afghan was placed in perfect order on the seat. A coffee cup sat on a coaster near the chair. Ethan lay huddled beneath a thick quilt.

He was safe. And asleep.

He clutched a small, much-worn teddy bear in the crook of his arm. Amanda blinked away tears at the sight of her son clinging to the toy. They'd had no time to bring anything with them. She'd taken him away from everything he knew and loved. And Blake had provided Ethan a small bit of childhood to hold.

She had no doubt Blake had watched over Ethan after putting her to bed last night. The nightmares must have come. Again.

And she hadn't heard them. Blake had.

Slowly, she walked back to her bedroom to dress. God, how had this happened? All she'd wanted for Ethan was a good life, for him to feel safe and protected.

She wished she could ask Blake for help. Her heart had gone pitter-patter the few times he'd smiled. When he'd held her in his arms last night, he'd made her feel small, but not vulnerable. Only protected. For a second, she'd wanted to lean her head against him and forget the danger. But she had no choice. She had to hide the car she'd stolen and vanish under the radar. She couldn't ask a sheriff to break the law for her. Especially one who had been through what Blake had.

Amanda left the bedroom and headed toward the kitchen. Keeping as quiet as possible, she opened the door and stepped onto the porch. The sun's brightness made the ice sparkle like glistening diamonds. The place looked like a winter wonderland. One thing about West Texas, if you wanted the weather to change, all you had to do was wait a minute.

The ditch to her right wasn't deep, but last night it

might just as well have been the Grand Canyon. She shivered. She could have easily frozen to death.

She followed the line of the driveway as it curved in front of the small barn. Where had the car landed? She remembered hitting the brakes and skidding. Then little else. Shoving her hands into her pockets, Amanda crossed the yard and stared in disbelief at the scars marring the ice-covered snow on the road.

The car was gone.

She whirled around and ran into a wall of muscle.

Blake clasped her shoulders to steady her. "In a hurry?"

"Where's the car?" Oh, God. That beat-up station wagon was the only way out of town and into oblivion. Her hands trembled. Her money. The gun. Gone.

"Amanda." Blake shook her gently. "What's wrong with you?"

"Where. Is. The. Car?" She tried to keep the panic out of her voice, but she couldn't stop it from quivering.

"Scooter towed it to his garage. It's probably totaled."

"This can't be happening." Amanda's legs wobbled beneath her. What was she going to do? "Please tell me it's drivable."

"Your suspension is damaged. The tire was practically bent underneath."

"How much to fix it?"

"At least a thousand. Maybe more."

Amanda swayed. She could have crumpled into a heap on the snow and cried. She needed that car. But she had only a couple hundred in her purse.

Her purse. Her ID. Panic vibrated through her body. She had a vague memory of grabbing the bag as she stumbled out of the car, but had she? If the Austin cops found the car… "I've got to get Ethan. We have to go."

She started to run to the house, but her feet slipped on the ice, and she landed hard on her backside. The fall jarred her ribs. Fire seared through her. She doubled over and clutched at the wound, rocking to and fro. She couldn't stop the moans.

How could she protect her son like this?

Blake knelt beside her and pulled her into his arms. "Whoa, there. Take it easy. You're trying to foul up my bandage again."

She shoved herself to her feet, barely able to stand the burning at her side. She teetered, fighting against the spots dancing in front of her eyes. She couldn't pass out. "We have to disappear. He'll find us."

"Who's looking for you, Amanda?" He clasped her arms and spun her around to face him, his Stetson not shielding the intensity of his gaze.

"I don't know. And that's no lie. Some guy outside Vince's house shot me. He came after us. He won't stop. I know it. I have to get us out of here."

"I did a little research. There's no news of Vince being killed. Anywhere."

Amanda dug her fingers into Blake's arm. "Please tell me you didn't call Austin."

Before he could answer, she wrenched away, struggled up the front steps and stumbled through the door. Blake followed, hovering beside her like an overprotective guardian. She knew he wouldn't give up, but he'd have to. She'd beg, borrow or steal some money. Pay him back later. Somehow. Ethan's room drew her gaze. The door stood open.

Her son hadn't made a move without her since Vince's death. What if the killer had found them? What if he'd taken her son?

She ran across the hardwood floor and rushed into the bedroom. Empty. "Ethan!"

Fear laced her voice. She whirled around, shoved open the closet.

No Ethan. "Where is he?" She searched the bathroom. Behind the shower curtain. Nothing.

"Oh, God, Blake. Where's Ethan?"

Blake didn't respond. She looked over her shoulder. He stood frozen, staring at a cracked-open entrance to a room down the hall. His face turned white. "No."

Blake burst into a run and slammed open the oak door against the wall. Amanda ran into his back.

"What are you doing?" Blake's voice boomed. "No one goes in here."

Ethan froze, the bright yellow dump truck in his hand rolling to a stop. Amanda placed herself between Ethan and a livid Blake. She'd never seen him like this.

"You...you can't play with that." Agony carved into each line of his face, he sidestepped Amanda and took the truck from Ethan.

Terror painted her son's expression. "I'm sorry. I'm sorry. I'm sorry." He ran to Amanda and threw himself against her.

She winced as he hit her side, but banished the waves of pain, focused solely on Ethan. "Shh, honey. Mommy's here." Worry vanished. She glared at Blake. "What are you trying to do? Scare him to death?"

Blake's wild-eyed gaze darted around the room before slowly clearing. He stared at the dog, who cowered in the corner, at Amanda holding her son. His throat spasmed. He thrust a shaking hand through his hair. "Oh, my God. I—"

The torment on Blake's face shattered her.

He stared down at the floor behind her. She followed

his gaze. A cardboard box in the middle of the floor. The name *Joey* in large bold letters on its side. And she understood. His son's toys. And from the look of dust covering the furniture, the door hadn't been opened since Blake had moved here.

A twin bed with a football bedspread lay untouched, waiting for someone.

The room was a shrine.

"Blake—"

His distraught stare met hers. "I'm…sorry. I haven't been in here since—" His voice trailed off. He turned and slowly walked out. His shoulders slumped, as if his soul had broken in two.

She stared after him. Her heart shattered at the devastation and loss on his face. Her eyes stung at the defeated picture of his leaving the room.

She rubbed her face. What had she done? Ethan was close to Joey's age when he'd been killed. She hadn't considered how hard this would be for Blake. The painful memories Ethan would trigger. She'd never wanted to hurt Blake. She'd never knowingly have done that.

Blake's steps faded, and Amanda knelt down on the floor, needing to touch Ethan, to remind herself he was alive and here. She pulled him into her lap and cupped his face. She pushed back the hair falling on his forehead. What if she'd lost her son as Blake had lost his? Would she survive?

Ethan's face scrunched up. "I didn't mean to do anything bad."

"I know, honey, I know. What made you come in here?"

"Just looking. Sheriff Blake found the bear in a box in my closet. I saw all the stuff in here…" His voice trailed off.

Amanda studied the boxes in the room, brand-new with shipping labels still intact. Left here to wait. For a boy to play with them. A boy who never came.

Until yesterday. Until Ethan.

"You wanted more toys?"

He nodded, his expression full of chagrin. "I just wanted to play. I didn't mean to make him mad."

Struggling to keep the pain she felt for Blake off her face, she kissed her son's forehead, her resolve to protect him that much stronger. "He wasn't mad. Just surprised." She pushed back on her heels. "Why don't you play in your room for a while, and I'll talk to Blake."

A gruff throat clearing from the doorway drew her gaze. Blake's eyes looked bloodshot, but he forced a smile on his face and knelt down.

"I'm sorry, Ethan. I didn't mean to scare you."

With a shaking hand, Blake passed the yellow truck to her son. "This was my little boy, Joey's, favorite toy. I think he'd like you to have it."

"Joey?" Ethan's face screwed up in thought. "Uncle Vince said Joey's in the clouds."

Blake's jaw throbbed with the struggle to keep himself in check. He nodded.

"I wish he was here," Ethan said.

"So do I."

Amanda could see Blake was close to the breaking point. "How about I cook everyone breakfast?" she said brightly.

"Bacon?" Ethan asked, the word cautious and hopeful.

She looked at Blake. He gave a slight nod, his expression haunted.

"Sounds good, sweetie. You go play in the living room."

Ethan walked to the door. He paused and turned to Blake. "I wish you had a green tractor like my friend Billy, only little, but I'll take good care of the truck. I promise."

"Thank you," Blake said softly. He reached out to Ethan, but then pulled his hand back.

Ethan hugged the yellow toy to his body and disappeared into the hallway.

Amanda turned to Blake. "I'm—"

"Don't. I shouldn't have yelled. It won't happen again."

"You made it okay. That truck means more than you know. He bonded with one of the construction workers who took him for a ride on a green tractor." Hesitantly, she stepped toward him. "Blake, I just wanted to say I can tell you were a wonderful father. I'm so sorry for your loss."

"Yeah." He backed away and tugged at the football bedspread, his look bleak. "This was my room when I was a kid. Mom and Dad had it ready for Joey whenever he visited. They'd updated everything right before…" Blake's voice trailed off. "He never…"

She crossed toward him and soothed him with a tentative touch. When Blake didn't pull away, she squeezed his solid arm and looked at him, her eyes burning, his face swimming as she gazed at him through her tears. "I saw you with Joey. I came to you because I knew if anything happened to me, you'd protect Ethan." She bit her lip. "You're the only person I can say that about."

His hand covered hers. "If you'll trust me, Amanda, I can help." He cleared his throat. "I promise to protect you and your son."

"I know. You're one of the few people who can understand what I'm facing now." She studied the strain behind his eyes, the tightness of his mouth. "Help me disappear. It's what Vince would've wanted."

Blake stiffened and removed her hand from his arm. "Don't mention his name, Amanda."

Fool. Why had she said that? She had to make him appreciate what was at stake. Amanda closed her eyes. Should she tell him? Was it the only way to make him understand? The only way to convince him to help her vanish?

She drew in a slow, deep breath and lifted her chin, praying for courage, hoping she was doing the right thing. "You have to listen to me, Blake."

He shot her a skeptical look. She could tell he was ready to turn away.

"Vince was devastated when we heard the news about Kathy and Joey," she rushed. "You didn't see what it did to him. He changed. He avoided me and Ethan. I didn't know why."

"Showing his true colors." Blake bit out the words through clenched teeth.

"He loved Ethan. I spent eighteen hours in that car trying to figure out why Vince acted the way he did. And why he was murdered. I realized ever since Joey was killed, Vince has been hiding something. From me, from you, from everyone."

"The fact that he was a cop on the take?"

"No! When I was forced to move in with him because of the debts Carl had racked up, Vince was furious, even though he'd made the offer the year before. He wanted me out of the house fast, but he also made me take self-defense classes. He taught me escape routes. I thought he wanted me safe from Carl. Now I recognize Vince knew it was dangerous for us to be with *him*. Not because of my ex, but because of the men *you* suspected."

"At least he had some sense of honor and responsibility."

Amanda ignored the bitterness in Blake's voice. "Vince said you'd been through enough. That you'd already paid too high a price for being a good cop." Her eyes burned with compassion. "I don't think he was talking about losing your job."

He froze and clasped her by the shoulders. "What are you saying?"

She wrapped her arms around her body. "If you don't let Ethan and me go, I'm certain we'll have an 'accident,' too." Amanda paused. "Like Kathy and Joey."

Blake's expression turned deadly, his eyes narrowed and cold. "Are you telling me Kathy and Joey's car wreck wasn't an accident?"

"I don't have proof, but I can't take the chance. I'm desperate. Ethan saw the killer. He's gone after us once. We have to leave before anyone else dies."

His face had gone gray as death. He reeled from her and sank into Joey's bed, staring up at her. "They were murdered?"

Chapter Three

"We've got a problem with the sister and the kid."

The words spoken through the lieutenant's prepaid cell phone made him frown. He rose from his desk and shoved his arms into his old leather jacket, irritated he couldn't wear the winter coat that cost more than his colleagues made in a year. Maybe two. These days, though, he couldn't be too careful. He exited the police station and rounded a corner. Damn it all. His entire setup was imploding. Millions of dollars still to be had and Vince had ruined everything.

"Talk."

"The car she ripped off just popped up on a plate check." The man at the other end paused. "In Carder, Texas."

The lieutenant punched the brick wall of the station. "I knew that bastard Vince was working with Blake all along. I should've killed them both."

Redmond had been too goody-goody to make it in the big city. He'd never understood how to the play the game.

He'd talked too much, though. Enough that a convenient accident to the whistle-blowing cop would've started an investigation. Until his family had been killed—accidentally, of course. Still, it had taken his father's death—accidental, of course—for Blake to drop everything, pack his bags and crawl back to the Podunk town where he belonged.

The lieutenant frowned. Convenient. Well-planned. But stupid. Well, mistakes could be rectified and learned from. "Get to Carder. Vince *must* have sent the evidence there. Find it, then kill them. I want Vince's family eliminated, and I want Blake Redmond silenced once and for all."

A slight pause over the phone spoke volumes.

"You have a problem with that?"

"Even the boy?"

The tentative voice set his teeth on edge. Was the man getting squeamish?

"Especially the boy. He's the only witness. If you don't want to end up in jail with some of the perps you put there, do the job right."

"Hey, Lieutenant."

He glanced up at a cheerful greeting and waved at the cop moving past the alley before returning to the conversation. "Any questions?"

"No, sir."

"Johnson? Be smart. You screw this up, you'll end up worse than Redmond. You'll know why your family died."

BLAKE'S KNEES GAVE WAY. He dropped to the bed Joey had never slept in. He couldn't think, couldn't process. His thoughts whirled and his hands shook. Not with fear, with fury. Could Kathy and Joey really have been murdered? Because of *his* questions, *his* investigation?

The truth exploded into rage. He'd wanted to be a cop all his life. Justice. Duty. Honor. He'd believed in the hype. He'd lived it. It was in his blood. Could his son have died because of the life Blake had chosen?

More than that. If Amanda was right, his *partner* had known. Vince, Blake's so-called best friend, had known—or at least suspected—what had happened. He'd let Blake come back to Carder unaware, let those murderers run free.

Bastard.

Every instinct screamed at Blake to hightail it to Austin and rip apart his old police command center until he learned the truth. If they'd killed Kathy and Joey, he'd make whoever was involved pay. No matter the cost.

"Blake?"

He looked up at Amanda. Her voice quivered. Her deep blue eyes were filled with concern, pity...and something else. Fear?

He averted his gaze and stared down at his hands. His knuckles were white. His fists trembled as wrath consumed him. He wanted to yell and scream, release the overwhelming anger that shook his soul.

"Vroom."

The small rumbling sound filtered from the other room. Ethan. Blake blinked. He couldn't scare the boy again. Control. He had to regain control. He took a long, shuddering breath. Then another.

The police radio squawked to life from the other room. "Blake, it's Parris. That car Scooter towed. I just ran the plates. It was stolen."

The words wrenched Blake out of the quicksand of emotions he'd been sinking into. He rose from Joey's bed and looked at Amanda in disbelief. Her face paled. In guilt.

Unbelievable.

Helping her just got a lot more complicated.

He crossed the floor to her. "Grand theft auto? A felony? What were you thinking? When you took that car, you tied my hands."

"Why'd your deputy have to run the plates? You ruined everything."

"Don't put this on me. As far as Parris understood, the vehicle was abandoned. Standard procedure."

"And you're just so danged efficient here in Carder, huh?"

Blake shoved his hand through his hair. She'd broken the law, even though she'd had a damn good reason. He enforced the law, but justice was supposed to be black and white. There were too many blasted shades of gray here. He hated the gray.

She didn't back away but met his gaze. "Oh yeah, making life harder for you is *just* what I planned. The guy who shot me was chasing us. He knew the make, model and plates. The bullet holes and busted windows were a dead giveaway. I had to take that car. What was I supposed to do? Call the cops?"

He understood. She didn't know who she could trust in Austin. He didn't, either. Blake cursed. She should have trusted him, though. She should have told him the truth the moment she regained consciousness.

He needed time to think. He couldn't pull in his staff or state contacts. He stalked into the living room, picked up the receiver and pressed the button.

She raced after him and gripped his arm. "Please," she whispered.

He glared at her. Damn her for believing he'd put her or Ethan at risk.

"Got the message, Parris. I'll get back to you. Redmond out." With a quick flick he turned down the volume on the receiver and faced Amanda. "You've put me in a tough spot."

"I know I can't stay here," she said. "With the plates on record, it's only a matter of time before they find us. Please, Blake, forget you ever saw us. Let me disappear."

Anxiety coated her face and radiated from her voice. Her entire body tensed. She was ready to run. He hated the look, the sound of her fear. Hated Vince for pulling her into his mess, and that the man responsible wasn't around to point the finger at the bad guys.

"Austin is five hours away—in good weather. Get Ethan some breakfast, and we'll come up with a plan."

"But—" She hesitated, a furtive glance toward the outside door, then the kitchen.

He sighed and placed his hands on her slight shoulders, resisting the urge to pull her against him, to comfort her...to lose himself in her touch. He buried the yearning. "Give me time to figure out how to help you without us all ending up in jail."

He waited, half expecting her to challenge him again. Her questioning blue gaze studied him, as if she were trying to read his heart. He didn't want her to look too closely. She'd shaken him to the core with her suspicions about his family's death. He may very well have failed them in more ways than he'd ever imagined.

He couldn't fail her and Ethan, too. He wouldn't.

With a light touch of her hand on his arm, she nodded, called out to Ethan and led him, still clutching the toy truck, into the kitchen. At least occasionally she knew when not to push.

Blake shrugged into his shearling coat and tugged down his Stetson, ignoring the fresh wave of grief that threatened to wash over him. He'd survived Joey's death knowing that accidents happen. But murder... Blake shoved the thought away. One fact remained: Amanda had been shot. She and Ethan were terrified.

He couldn't let himself get distracted. Not now.

Leo sat near the kitchen door, watching him. He detoured and grabbed his weapon as the crackle of frying bacon filtered through his house. Almost made the place homey, but Blake couldn't indulge in that dream.

He poked his head into the kitchen. "I'll be in the barn," he said, ignoring the familial picture of Amanda at the stove, Ethan playing at her feet. "I've turned on the intercom. It's voice-activated, so I'll hear you if you need me."

He had to find focus and clarity. For Kathy and Joey's memory. For Ethan and Amanda's safety.

Leo followed him out of the kitchen, his tail down, whining. "Stay." The dog's ears sank and Blake patted the animal's head. "Guard."

Alert, Leo headed back into the kitchen, giving Blake some piece of mind. The dog could have been a K-9. He was a born watchdog, and Blake needed all the help he could get.

Amanda was right about one thing: once Parris had run the plates, the fuse had been lit. As Blake stepped on the yard, the crisp cold was no longer dangerous. The winter sun was brighter than usual. Before long, the ice would be gone, and travel would get back to normal. The perps would come to Carder. To find her and kill her. She was unfinished business.

By sending Amanda here, Vince had brought murderers to Blake's town. If these cops had also killed his family, they would use anyone and do anything to get what they wanted. Which put Carder, and particularly his mom, the last of his family, at risk. At least she'd moved into town after his father died, unable to bear living in their ranch house. She'd be a little harder to track down, but not impossible.

He had to find a way to protect them all without bending the rules and becoming the cops he despised.

His feet crunched along the grass as he headed toward the barn. The moment he walked in, the ornery horse his father had loved for his wild and fiery temper started up. The chestnut danced around, flicked his head and glared at Blake. The SOB would bite anyone else who came near him. Even worse after his father died.

After a half hour of mindless chores, regret and strategizing, Blake knew he couldn't avoid the stallion any longer. He grabbed a flake of hay and eased toward the stall. The animal puffed a breath through his nose and rose on his hind legs, batting the air.

"He looks dangerous." Amanda's whisper filtered from behind.

Blake's heart skipped a beat at her voice. Utter aloneness had settled over him like a soggy, woolen blanket in this barn full of memories. The loss. The grief. Now, something inside of him longed to touch her, to turn to her. He'd wanted to hold her for longer than he cared to admit. He knew what her lips tasted like. He remembered so clearly when he'd come upon her under the mistletoe two years ago. Vince had egged him on, and she'd blushed, smiling, closing her eyes for a friendly kiss that had turned into so much more. When Blake had lowered his mouth to hers, the electricity between them knocked him over. He'd wrapped his arms around her. She'd parted her mouth under his.

Only the whoops and hollers had stopped him from sweeping her into a bedroom. One look at Vince's dark expression, though, and Blake had pushed the episode aside. He should do the same thing now. His first duty was to protect her and her son, not succumb to long-denied desires.

"He *is* dangerous. He doesn't like strangers." Blake shifted his body between her and Sugar. "Where's Ethan?"

"Asleep," she said softly, eyeing the snorting horse. "He just nodded off. I'm glad. He needed the rest. He didn't get much on the drive here."

"Or last night."

Blake studied her every movement, the straightening of her spine, the flash of frustration in her eyes, the challenging tilt of her chin.

"You could've left me with him. I'd have taken care of him."

"You needed the rest, too." Blake took in the dark circles under her eyes, but he couldn't let sympathy derail him. She hadn't been honest. She had to start. He needed to know more. "Ethan screamed in his sleep."

She jerked her head up, then rubbed the bridge of her nose. The bravado seeped out of her. Her cobalt eyes shone with unshed tears.

"He screamed in his sleep last night," Blake repeated. "About Vince."

"I didn't hear him." She leaned against the wall. "He won't talk about it. Not one word about who killed Vince. I don't even know for sure if Ethan saw the murderer."

Vulnerability poured from her. Blake understood the helpless feeling all too well, but he wouldn't keep the truth from her. "From what he murmured in his sleep, I think he witnessed everything. Vince told Ethan to hide," Blake said. "Your brother probably saved Ethan's life."

Blake hated to concede the truth. If nothing else,

Vince had tried to protect his own family. Just no one else's.

"Vince was a good man, Blake. I know you don't believe that right now, but he was."

"He lied to me about how my family died."

At the sound of his raised voice, Sugar rammed against his stall with an infuriated whinny.

Amanda jumped back and stumbled against a saddle. The stirrup swung as she caught herself.

"Get away from there. He goes crazy if anyone touches Dad's saddle. Go to the other side of the aisle."

"What's wrong with him?" she asked.

"He killed my father."

She gasped but didn't leave. She shifted, clearly ill at ease, and licked her lips. "Why would you care for an animal that hurt you so badly?"

Blake studied the horse, trying not to let his gaze linger on the slight parting of her mouth. "I'm not sure. It just doesn't feel right to blame him. Sugar hasn't been the same since he kicked Dad in the head. The vet suggested we put him down. Mom couldn't do it, so I keep him. I'm the only one he'll let ride him these days." The horse snorted and glared at Blake, pawing at the gate. "Will you just go until I figure out our next move? I'm in as good a mood as Sugar."

"You care about him despite what he did?" Her voice was curious, with a hint of challenge.

Blake could see where she was going. He thought for a moment. "He always had a bad temper, but he was proud, confident. We think he was spooked during a storm and struck out blindly. Now he's got an edge to him. Anger, fear, regret. Maybe that's why I can't put him down."

"Maybe Vince deserves the same benefit of the doubt."

Blake threw the hay into the stall. "Have at it, Sugar." The horse gave the feed a disdainful look. "Yeah, I know. Oats, too. Dad spoiled you." Blake mixed the delicacy. The greedy animal watched, but Blake could have sworn the beast kept his eye on Amanda, too. Just as he knew Amanda was watching him.

He turned and crossed the aisle to stand so near her that he could study any small change in her expression. He tilted his Stetson. "At least Sugar shows remorse. Vince never did."

Pain flashed in her eyes and a slight wince twisted her lips. "You're wrong."

He ignored the small intake of breath, the delicacy of her skin, even the slight blush in her cheeks almost hidden by the wild curl of her auburn hair.

"It doesn't matter now. Life goes on, and you deal with it. My priorities are to keep you, Ethan and my town safe, find out the truth about my family and bring the guilty to justice. No more. No less."

He backed away from temptation, from the ache to touch and play with those curls, just to see if she still smelled of jasmine, and if his body still leaped to attention at the scent.

Sugar whinnied, and Blake reached into his pocket for a lump of sugar. He eased over to the stall and stuck his hand in, palm flat. "You bite me, and it's over."

As if Sugar knew Blake was serious, he snatched the treat and paced.

"If you want to protect me, then help me leave. Help me disappear." She reached for Blake's arm and tugged at his coat. Her hand brushed his. She didn't understand how his skin could be warm when her body shivered with cold, clear to the bone. She quaked in the flimsy coat. "Please. For Ethan."

She leaned closer and met his gaze, trying to read his intentions, trying to ascertain how much she could count on him. He shrugged out of his sheepskin, and with unbelievably gentle hands, wrapped the warm, wool-lined jacket around her. She had to sigh as Blake's own heat seeped into her skin from the lining, like a cocoon of protection. She wanted to close her eyes and lean on him, to let Blake take over. She'd wanted his embrace since that mind-blowing kiss that Christmas Eve. Her knees trembled and she clutched at him. He clasped her arms in his warm hands, his gaze compelling her to look at him. The gold flecks in his hazel eyes burned hot with intensity. And something else. Something she'd thought she'd never see again. Desire.

"You don't have to face this alone." His voice had gone low as he stared her down. His breath caught. The awareness dancing between them sparked to life.

Her heart fluttered in response to his nearness. She could feel the heat radiating from him. Not only from his body, but also from his gaze. Why was this happening to her?

She wanted nothing from him except a way to run.

Instead, her lips tingled, wanting to be tasted. She licked them, and he let out a small moan. He cupped her cheek and tugged at the auburn curls that had escaped from their clip. Gently, he pushed her hair from her face. "Did I ever tell you that you're beautiful?"

"Blake—"

"No, I wouldn't have. You were forbidden fruit."

He leaned in slowly, giving her plenty of time to resist him, but she couldn't back away. No matter what her mind screamed, her instincts kept her feet firmly planted. "This is a bad idea. There's too much going on. It's not real." The pulse in his throat throbbed, and a whiff of pine from his cologne tickled her nostrils. Her favorite. Did she love that scent because Blake had always worn it? "I have to disappear. I can't stay."

Her heart pounded in anticipation even as she uttered the halfhearted resistance.

"I always wondered," he whispered, "if you really tasted as good as I remembered. Christmas sweet and spice." He rubbed his thumb on her lower lip. "May I?"

She didn't think, just nodded her head.

With a deep groan, he tugged her into his arms and took her lips with a force that made her whimper. No one had ever kissed her like he was too hungry to let her go.

He wrapped her in his arms and when he pressed her lips open, she gladly let him in. He was right. She'd wondered if the kiss had been a fluke for longer than she'd wanted to admit. She pressed closer to him, her breasts crushing against his broad chest.

Heat sprang between them, and her body sizzled with want. Low in her belly, the recognition of her yearning for this man kindled something she hadn't felt in too long.

No fluke. She let herself sink into the feelings. She wanted so much to let him lay her down in this hay and make the world go away. Erase everything that had happened. She felt at home in his arms.

Amanda rubbed her hands over the strength of his muscles, the broadness of his shoulders, the narrowness at his waist. His response to her touch was primal and immediate. She could feel his hardness grow against her belly.

He wanted her. As much as she wanted him.

A loud car horn sounded from the driveway. Amanda couldn't stop the thud of her heart. Her knees shook as she tried to steady herself. She would have let him take her. Here in the barn. This wasn't good. She wrenched her mouth from beneath Blake's and pushed him away. "Oh, God, have they found us?"

"Stay here. I'm not expecting anyone." Blake pulled a Glock off the tackbox and strode to the barn door. He cursed. "It's my deputy, Parris. Keep out of sight."

Amanda knelt near the door and peeked out. The older man had stopped not far from where her car had skidded. He knelt down and studied the ground. Hopefully he wouldn't find anything. The melting ice and the tow should have destroyed any footprints.

Another reason to leave, despite the kiss. She touched her fingers to her tender lips. Blake's touch had been everything she'd fantasized. Another memory to keep her warm at night when she was alone.

Blake reached Parris, and Amanda strained to hear. "What're you doing here?"

"Scooter called me about the car I ran. He found a bloody scarf and a gun on the front seat." Parris rose and slapped his hat on his thigh. "The station wagon was stolen from an Austin bar. Not too far from where you used to work." He crossed his arms. "You didn't patrol last night. You asked me to check on your mama. For the first time ever. Wanna tell me what's going on?"

The deputy stood toe-to-toe with Blake. The man had guts. Even from here, Amanda could see Blake's posture straightening, his stance threatening. She'd run the other way if he ever looked at her like that.

Blake leaned forward and said something pointed and short to the deputy, who stood firm, his expression mutinous.

Not a good sign.

Finally, the man nodded stiffly, got back into his car and took off. Amanda let out the breath she'd been holding. What had Blake told him? Too much? She waited until the deputy's car had turned off the road and disappeared from sight before she stood.

Blake returned to the barn and nodded at a speaker on the barn wall. "Ethan wake up?"

"Not a peep. Even your dog didn't bark."

"Leo knows a friend when he sees one."

"Is Parris a friend?"

"My dad's best friend since they were kids. And a good deputy."

"Which means I have to worry about him."

"He's loyal. He's taking care of a job for me." Blake's expression had closed off—stubborn and oh-so-stoic. He was hiding something. She recognized the signs. He and Vince were so alike.

"Is he checking up on me?"

"You don't trust me at all, do you?"

"I know what I'm asking." She touched her lower lip. "It's gotten complicated, hasn't it?"

His eyes flared as he focused on her mouth. "I want you safe, but the moment you told me about my family you changed the game. Because now we know they'll kill the innocent to get what they want. You'll never be safe."

Blake's words slapped her, but she knew he was right. "Does Parris know I'm here?"

"He's suspicious. You jacked the car from Austin. You came here. Your blood will place you in the car. A gun was on the seat. Probably with your prints on it. Am I right?"

Amanda nodded.

"Please don't tell me it's Vince's gun."

When he said it like that, the reality of her situation made her tremble. They could use the facts against her. She'd taken a gun from a crime scene. They could tie her back to Vince's murder. What had she done?

Blake shook his head, almost in disbelief. "The evidence is stone cold, Amanda. What am I supposed to do about that? The only thing keeping a warrant from being issued right now is you took your purse last night. I found it in the ditch."

The ringing of his cell phone echoed through the barn.

"Redmond." He listened and his lips grew tight. "When?"

Blake's sharp question made Amanda's insides quake.

"You get the plate?" he asked. He let out a low whistle. "Rental. Coordinate with Parris. I'll leave him instructions."

"What—" Amanda began.

Blake held up his hand and pressed a button on his phone. "Parris, it's Blake. Don't wait. Get over to Mom's house now. Take her to the rendezvous point. Coordinate with Smithson."

No. This couldn't be happening. They'd found them. Amanda headed toward the barn door.

"My father was your best friend. Trust me," Blake said. "I'll be in touch."

She paused and stared after him. What did she think he was doing?

"I'll send the horses into the pasture. Get the Collins kid to corral them up. Except Sugar. But only after you check things out. And Parris, don't trust *anyone* asking about me or that car Scooter's got." He paused. "Especially cops."

He snapped the phone closed. "We're out of time. Someone must've taken a plane or been halfway here already. Deputy Smithson stopped two strangers speeding like idiots on these icy roads. Austin cops heading toward town. They could be here any minute."

Amanda's heart sank. She should never have come to Blake. "Ethan!"

She raced to the barn door, Blake beside her. Just as they reached the opening, a car careened down the driveway and skidded to a halt. Blake wrapped his arm around Amanda's waist, stopping her momentum. She cried out in pain. He loosened his grip and tugged her back into the building just as two men jumped out, their faces hidden by ski masks.

A spray of gunfire peppered the barn.

Her side burning like fire, Amanda struggled against Blake. She had to get to the house. "Ethan."

"You'll be dead two steps out the door," he hissed in her ear. He grabbed her and settled her in the corner of a stall, then palmed his Glock. "You know how to shoot this?"

"Vince trained me."

"I don't have an extra clip." He handed her the weapon. "Fifteen rounds. Make every shot count."

"What are you going to do?"

"Get Ethan."

Amanda grasped the gun confidently and released the safety before pointing the barrel to the ground.

"Like a pro. I should've known." He smiled at her, the deadly smile of a man going into battle. "Keep them occupied. I'll make my way around back. Grab Ethan. We'll leave in the old truck. Be ready."

"That bucket of bolts at the side of the barn? Does it even run?"

"You'd be surprised." Blake clasped her fingers in his. "You can do this. I'll be back with Ethan."

"We'll never outrun them."

He smiled, his expression devilish. "You let me take care of that."

A flicker of hope flared in her chest. He had a plan.

"I'll bring your son back to you. I promise."

She bit her lip and nodded.

"When I give you the signal, take two or three shots."

Blake stacked several hay bales against the wall of the barn as a barricade, then slid aside two small pieces of wood. One left a hole just large enough for a gun. The other was at spotting height.

"You can't be serious?"

"What can I tell you? My buddies and I played Alamo when I was a kid." His voice turned quiet, his expression serious. "Amanda, unlike in history, I always won."

Blake snagged the weapon from her hands, went to the door and took two shots. He handed the gun back to her. "Go! Shoot!"

Amanda clasped the weapon in her hands, fell onto the hay and squeezed off three more rounds through the hole.

Blake leaped out the barn door and raced across the yard. To her horror, one of the men noticed him. He shifted his aim toward Blake's running figure.

"Blake!" she screamed and pulled the trigger.

Chapter Four

Amanda's warning scream sent Blake diving for the porch. The bullet whizzed past his ear, the high-pitched sound riding a hot puff of air. Damn, that was close. His shoulder hit the frozen ground, and he rolled over with a grunt to peer across the yard from behind the wooden slats.

The Glock thundered another shot as Amanda squeezed the trigger. One of the men yelped and grabbed his arm. "Good job, honey," Blake whispered. She knew how to handle that gun. Better than most. "Thank you, Vince."

"Blake!" she shouted. "Are you okay?"

"Fine! Keep shooting."

He hoped she recognized his words were for their assailants more than her. He didn't want them to know she was down to her last ten bullets.

A shot slapped near his head. Good. He'd diverted some of their attention from her. He changed positions and stood, out of the line of sight of their ambush, but visible to her. He could make out her sag of relief.

Once she saw him, she refocused on the men behind the car. Another bevy of shots whizzed past him. He was running out of time. Blake raced around the back of the house and tried the knob. The brass wouldn't give.

Locked. Just his luck. No time for subtlety. He kicked in the door and ran to Ethan's room.

Empty.

"Ethan. It's Sheriff Blake."

Silence.

The poor kid was probably hiding and traumatized, afraid to call out. Luckily, Blake could count on someone who wouldn't stay quiet. "Leo? Where are you, boy?"

The mutt let out a muffled bark from beneath the bed. Blake knelt down and found Ethan hiding his face in Leo's fur.

The dog licked the boy's hand, but Ethan shook his head and his grip tightened. "Have to hide," he muttered.

Blake wanted to grab the little boy, hug him and tell him everything would be all right. Problem was, he'd have been lying. "Stay here, Ethan. I'll be back for you," Blake promised. The boy was safe for now. "Watch out for him, mutt. I gotta create a distraction." He couldn't run across the yard like a carnival chicken with Ethan in his arms. Not without a fighting chance of getting to the barn alive.

Shots rang out again. The telltale sound of the Glock echoed. One more bullet down. The minute she ran out of ammo, the perps would kill her. He palmed the horse antibiotics from the spare room, then hurried into Joey's bedroom and ripped open one of the boxes of his toys. Blake shoved through the balls and games, ignoring the waves of emotion threatening to drown him. He couldn't afford to get lost in the memories inundating him. He had to stay focused. He needed to find Joey's last Christmas present.

Where had he put it? The packing had been a blur.

He'd thrown items in boxes trying not to think. He shoved aside two more boxes and a tall one loomed from the center of the room. He remembered putting toys in there. Joey had barely had a chance to play with the overabundance Blake had showered on his son that Christmas, trying to make up for too little time spent with him.

Blake tore at the taped lid of the cardboard box and dug through the toys and games. "Got 'em." He pulled out a ping-pong set, complete with two dozen balls.

He grabbed them and raced to the kitchen heading toward a rarely used drawer. Thank goodness for his mother. She believed no one should be without aluminum foil. Staying clear of the window, he counted another shot from the Glock. Damn.

Blake risked a quick look out the kitchen window. No clear shot from here. He couldn't see Amanda from this angle either, but she showed impressive discipline, firing just enough to keep the attackers pinned down.

He could kiss her again for being that smart—and that tough.

Moving fast and furious he snipped the ping-pong balls into shards with kitchen shears and used the foil to create three small bombs. Then he snagged a lighter. He ran to the living room and unlocked the gun cabinet. He grabbed extra clips for the Glock and his granddad's World War II Colt Model 1911. The .45 caliber bullets would blow a hole in anyone that tried to come after them.

He stuffed the clips into his pockets and the gun into the back of his jeans before running to Ethan's room.

No time to coax him. "Out, mutt," Blake ordered.

Leo scampered from beneath the mattress just as Blake reached under the bed and tugged Ethan by his jeans. He flipped the boy onto his back. The boy's eyes were squeezed shut, afraid to look. He whimpered in fear. Blake's heart twisted in agony. "Ethan, it's Sheriff Blake. Open your eyes. I'm taking you out of here."

The boy blinked through his blank stare. His clouded eyes cleared. "Mommy?"

"We're going to her." Blake plopped Ethan on his feet and zipped him into his coat. "You have to be brave right now. Do what I say."

"Have to hide. Uncle Vince said so."

Several loud cracks sounded from outside. Ethan shrank and tried to dive under the bed, but Blake hugged him tight. "Uncle Vince was right. Hiding is a good idea, but right now we have to get to your mom, okay, buddy?"

Ethan hesitated, looked up at Blake, and then nodded.

He grasped his truck in his hand. Blake looked at the yellow toy with a sigh. It was bulky, but the kid needed something to keep. "Good boy." He rose with Ethan in his arms. "Hold on tight to that truck. Leo, come."

The dog followed Blake to the back door. More cracks rang through the air. Blake set Ethan down and raised the bag. "Okay, buddy. See these? They're going to hide us, but I need you to do exactly what I tell you."

Ethan stuffed his thumb into his mouth and Blake let out a long stream of air. Most grown men wouldn't handle this kind of pressure. What could he expect from a five-year-old?

"Hold Leo's collar." Blake knew the mutt wouldn't move, but it would give Ethan something to hang on to. "I'm gonna light one of these. When it smokes, I'll come back and get you. Then we go to Mommy. Okay?"

Amanda's son bit his lip and grabbed the leather around the dog's neck.

"It's important, Ethan. Don't move until I say."

He nodded.

Blake stood. He could see Amanda's legs from this angle. She was focused. Good. No way could she help him get the hundred yards to the barn with boy and dog in tow. Except to continue firing.

Blake grabbed one of the makeshift bombs and lit the bottom. Once it caught fire, he ran out from behind the house and set it down.

Within seconds, white smoke poured from the opening of the foil funnel. The shots stopped momentarily.

"Can you see Redmond?" one of the men cursed.

More shots rang out. A flurry of four pops from the barn peppered near the guys' feet. Those would be all but her last bullet. Blake had run out of time. He lit the other two bombs and grabbed Ethan under one arm so the boy was protected as much as possible from the sight of the gunfight. "Let's go, Leo."

The dog stayed at Blake's side. Timing was everything. He tossed the second bomb down just as the first petered out. Amanda's last shot rang out. Blake let loose the final bomb. Within seconds, he'd made it to the side of the barn and bundled Leo and Ethan into the truck.

"Stay on the floor, I'm getting your mom."

Ethan hugged Leo to him and buried his face in the animal's fur.

The smoke was dwindling, but there was still enough to distract. Blake raced for the barn door. When he entered, Amanda stood, her entire body shaking, an empty gun in her hand, her face pale.

"Ethan?"

"In the truck. Give me the gun."

Blake snapped in one of the extra clips he'd pocketed. He handed Amanda a set of keys and a wad of cash. "I'll cover you. If anything happens to me, take the truck. Disappear."

She stared at the money and stuffed it in her pocket. The color returned to her cheeks. Damn she was brave.

"Ready," she said.

"Go." Blake shot several rounds as Amanda raced out of the barn.

When she rounded the corner, he took aim at the intruders' tires. Two shots. Two flats. Then he looked at his Sheriff's SUV. He sighed. They could hot-wire it in seconds.

Two more shots, two more flats. Another hit to his budget he'd eat, but it should delay them for a while.

A wild set of whinnies escaped from the stalls. The horses. Sugar banged against the wooden slats. He opened up all the stalls except Sugar's and let out a roar.

"Get out of here!" he yelled. "Yah!"

The horses raced out of the barn toward the pasture. Blake opened Sugar's gate and the horse eyed him with suspicion.

"You, too, beast. Protect them."

As if the animal understood, Sugar raised his hooves in the air and galloped out the gate. Blake dived around the corner and ran to the now-idling truck. Amanda sat in the driver's seat.

"Scoot over," he said. "Lay down until we get clear."

She slipped across the torn vinyl and tried to comfort Ethan. Blake wrenched the old truck into gear. "Come on, baby," he coaxed. He pulled the truck around and behind the barn.

The gunshots had stopped. He tore across the alfalfa field to a section of old wooden fencing. Without hesitation he barreled through the planks.

In his rearview mirror he caught one the guys in the

ski masks kicking the flattened tire. The other limped toward the Sheriff's SUV. They'd be frustrated for a while. Blake stomped on the accelerator and headed toward the main road.

"You can get up now," he said.

Amanda rose, shoving her riotous curls out of her face. She reached down to the floorboard. "Ethan, want to sit with Mommy?"

The boy shook his head at Amanda, remaining huddled next to Leo at their feet, clutching the yellow truck.

Amanda shot Blake a concerned look. He didn't like the returned vagueness on the boy's face, but nothing would erase the fear until Blake could arrest the perps. "Leave him be. He feels safe."

She let a hand rest on Ethan's head before looking around them. "Where are we going?"

Blake eased his foot off the accelerator as he reached a bridge. He recognized the glisten of black ice. "Off the pavement for one thing."

He turned onto a dirt road that clearly hadn't seen traffic since the storm hit. The truck hit a pothole. Amanda yelped and clutched at her side.

"Sorry," he said. "Can you gut it out for a while longer?"

"If he can, I can." She nodded at Ethan who was whispering to Leo. "There were two of them this time," she said, her voice low.

"Only one attacked you in Austin?" Blake asked.

"I couldn't have fended off two."

"You held your own today. Good shot."

"I was lucky."

"You were smart. I was impressed. Learn how to take a compliment."

When she didn't respond, Blake stared out at the frostbitten landscape. "It was too easy," he mused.

"What are you talking about? We barely escaped," she hissed.

"They could've taken us out. They had the firepower. They knew my name, and I recognized the moves. Definitely Austin cops."

Amanda shivered in her seat as Blake sent her a sidelong glance. "They want you alive. For a while."

"They have a funny way of showing it." Her hand moved to her side.

"What do they want from you, Amanda?"

She bit her lip. "The guy who attacked me said something about Vince's file. He tried to bargain with me. Our lives for the file." She paused. "I didn't believe him."

"Evidence," Blake surmised. "What was Vince up to?"

The truck hit a large dirt pothole, and Amanda whimpered. "I don't know, but he never gave me anything."

Blake steered around the next hole in the road. "Well, we know one thing. We've got to find that file. Before they do."

AMANDA SHIVERED in the frigid cold of the old truck, wrapping Blake's coat tighter around her as he dialed a number on his cell phone. Leo warmed her lower legs, so she knew Ethan wouldn't be chilled. She had no idea how long they'd driven, and she wouldn't mind continuing all the way to Mexico—if that's where Blake headed—except that every bounce on the road made her side burn. She could live with the hurt. Each slice of pain was proof they were alive. Blake had saved Ethan. Blake had saved her.

"No, I don't want to leave a message," Blake snapped into his cell phone. "I'll call back later."

He drummed his fingers on the steering wheel and glanced at the dashboard.

"Where are we going?" Amanda said.

"Not where I'd planned."

He glanced in the rearview mirror, pulled onto a dirt road and stopped the truck.

"What are you doing?"

"Keeping them from tracking us," he said. He dug his phone and a utility knife out of his pocket. With deft movements he opened the back of the phone, then removed the battery. He slipped the phone into his pocket. "Do you have a cell?"

She shook her head. "I lost it the night of the attack. Blake, what are we going to do?"

"For now, get off the road, hole up and figure out where that evidence is and how we can use it." He pulled onto the highway, executed a U-turn and hit another series of dirt roads.

Amanda was thoroughly lost in minutes. She sent a sidelong glance at Blake. A small puff of cold air escaped his mouth, but he didn't show any reaction to the cold, even though she snuggled in his sheepskin coat. Beneath his Stetson, his strong jaw held coiled tension and intensity. The gorgeous man sitting beside her could have posed for a picture next to the words *duty* and *honor.* If he committed to a woman or a cause, Amanda had no doubt he'd follow through. The realization lit a small tingle of hope. She was way out of her league. Could Blake find a way to help them?

The idea thrilled and scared her at the same time. Even now, she wanted to lean into his strong embrace and rest against the crook of his shoulder. She scanned his passionate and firm lips. She wanted another taste, another chance to feel the strength of his mouth parting hers, demanding, subduing. Another opportunity to feel held by a man who really could be in her corner. A man who could make a difference.

"You stare at me like that much longer, and I won't be responsible for my actions," he said, his voice husky.

Her face heated. "I...uh—"

One side of his full lips tilted up. "Don't worry, I won't act on the temptation. Yet." He paused. "We're almost there. See that windmill?"

The structure loomed in the distance, growing with every minute. As Blake's vehicle approached it, a large ranch house and a series of barns and pens rose above the icy ground. The place looked deserted.

"Who lives here?"

"The Maddoxes are visiting their granddaughter, who just had a baby. Their house is empty. Old man Maddox sold off most of his stock a few years ago. So no hands. Only thing we'll have to worry about is keeping out of sight of the kid who feeds what's left of the animals. We'll be safe here until I come up with a game plan."

"Are we really?" Amanda touched a shaking hand to Ethan's head. She didn't even ask him to take his thumb out of his mouth. How could she when she longed to take comfort in any scrap of hope. "I don't have what those guys want, and they want it bad. Can we ever be safe?"

He pulled around the back of the large ranch house and rumbled to a stop. Twisting toward her, he cupped her cheek and his gaze burned into hers. "Listen to me, Amanda. Trust me. I can help."

When she didn't answer, he sighed and opened the

door, his expression disappointed. "I'll check the place out. Wait here."

She believed Blake would do everything he could, but Vince had thought he could keep them safe as well. Look where good intentions got her brother.

As Blake circled the house, Ethan squirmed from the floorboard and peered out the windshield. He pointed to the farm equipment, sitting near a shed a ways away. "Look over there, Mommy. It's a tractor like Billy's." He twisted around. "There's a big cow behind that fence."

"It's a bull," Amanda said.

"This place is neat." Ethan scrambled toward the open door. His foot caught her side, and she gasped, waves of pain shooting through her.

"What happened?" Blake's sharp question out of nowhere had Ethan shrinking back against her.

She held her son next to her, and sucked in a soft breath, praying the wound hadn't started bleeding again. "It's nothing."

"The hell you say." He rounded the vehicle and opened the passenger door, lifting Ethan to the ground. Leo leaped out, and Blake leaned into Amanda. "How bad? Really?"

"It's fine."

"You're lying. You look ready to pass out." Blake whipped around as Ethan started across the field toward the large green tractor. "Son, this place isn't a playground and the tractor isn't a toy. Come with us."

The boy paused, clearly tempted.

"Ethan," Amanda called. "Mind Sheriff Blake."

With a long sigh, Ethan slunk back to the truck, his chin sagging as he kicked at the brown grass still laden with remnants of ice.

Blake handed Amanda Ethan's yellow truck, then

gently lifted her into his arms. She didn't protest. Her side burned like fire. She wrapped her arms around his neck.

"Why are you carrying Mommy?" Ethan asked, running up to them.

"She's tired," Blake said. "She's going to rest for a while."

"Mommies don't take naps." Ethan crossed his arms, so certain in his statement, Amanda bit back a smile in spite of the twinges.

Blake looked ready to spout off more orders, and she knew her son well enough to recognize the bit of stubbornness edging into his voice. She was surprised she hadn't seen this side of him sooner.

"I need to rest, honey. Okay?"

With a pout in his lip, Ethan nodded. Blake led them around to the front porch and snagged a key from above the jamb. After turning the lock and pushing through the door, he dumped the truck and house keys on the entryway table. He set her carefully on the overstuffed living room sofa before closing every drape and shutter in the room. "Keep that coat on," he told her as Ethan and Leo ran past. "I'll warm this place up, then we'll take a look."

Amanda rubbed her ungloved hands together and blew hot air into them to try to keep the circulation going as much as to distract herself. "How about a fire?"

Blake searched the wall for a thermostat and set it. "I don't want to use the woodstove. No need to advertise our presence with a smoke signal."

"Sorry," she muttered. "Stupid idea." She cursed herself for not thinking of the obvious. She'd have given them away for a little warmth.

He rounded on her. "You're not stupid. You're in a

strange situation, in a place you don't know. You were right. We need heat. Don't sell yourself short."

She warmed at his fierce defense but knew he was just being kind. She'd made some dumb decisions in her life. She looked at her son as he explored the corners of the living room, Leo by his side. Ethan was the best thing she'd ever done.

The furnace kicked on, and the comforting hum yanked her out of a path of self-doubt. She knew better than to continue on that road. She'd exited it when she'd left Carl, her ex, and his pseudo-criminal lifestyle. She refused to let herself get back on that highway.

"I'll search out the rooms and find Ethan a safe place to play while I look at your wound."

"That's not necessary."

"I can't risk an infection setting in. You shouldn't, either," he said, shooting her a frown before disappearing down the hallway.

Part of her wanted to thank him for taking charge, but she still bristled at his high-handed attitude. He was way too comfortable giving orders. She heard several doors opening and closing throughout the house.

"Blankets," Amanda called out, her teeth chattering. "We'll need them until the house warms up."

The moment she said the words, he appeared with a stack of hand-knitted afghans. He sent her an arrogant grin before turning to her son. "Ethan, I found a good place for you to camp out and play while your mom rests."

"I gotta take care of Mommy. I promised."

Amanda stood, unable to stop the wince. Blake was right, dang him. She walked over to Ethan and placed a kiss on his forehead before swiping at the errant strands of hair falling down his forehead. He'd seen too much.

It wasn't fair. "Sheriff Blake will take care of me, little man. I'll be in later to check on you."

"Can Leo play?" Ethan asked.

"He can do more than that. Leo, come," Blake ordered, carrying the truck. She followed as he led her son into a small bedroom and placed the toy on the floor. He wrapped an afghan around Ethan, then moved two chairs into place on either side of the boy. He threw another blanket over the chair backs and motioned the dog under the blanket.

"How about you and Leo camp out in here?"

The dog ducked under the makeshift tent, took a quick turn and pressed his furry body against Ethan's, licking his face. Her son hugged the dog tightly, but his face wasn't tense and afraid. Leo had comforted Ethan in a way she couldn't. That dog hadn't left the boy alone. Unlike her. One trip to the barn. One mind-blowing kiss, and Ethan had been trapped. No more. Every choice she made from now on would be all about keeping him safe.

He pulled the blanket over his head. A loud *vroom* sounded. Her son had gone into a world of make-believe.

Blake clasped her elbow and bent down, his mouth next to her ear. "Ethan will be fine. We'll be just around the corner. You'll hear him if he calls out."

She stared up at his strong figure and Blake held out a hand. He could take care of them. She could see it in his face, and she believed him.

He pointed to her side. "How's it feel?"

"It doesn't hurt now."

"So you wouldn't mind getting back in that truck and driving over potholes for another couple hours?"

"Of course not," she lied, dreading even the thought. To prove herself, she crossed her arms in front of her, and that small movement tugged on her wound.

He frowned down at her. "Forget this," he muttered and dragged her down the hall.

"Ouch. Cut it out."

"If that little movement hurt, then you lied to me." He pulled out the horse pills. "You're due. Someone needs to take care of you, because you don't seem to mind if you get an infection."

He led her into a large kitchen. Double burners and ovens. A huge butcher's block island. He banged open cabinets, searching for something. The slam made her flinch. For the first time she noticed the tension in his posture, his back, his neck. The hair that he'd obviously shoved his fingers through. He glanced at her over his shoulder, his eyes more than concerned, she realized with a flash of insight. He was worried about her.

Turning, he rifled through the cabinet above the stove.

"What are you looking for?"

"Something that will keep you out of the hospital until we can track down Vince's file."

"You really think we can find his evidence?"

He gave a satisfied grunt and grabbed medical supplies out of the cabinet. "If Vince wanted us to, yeah. If he didn't…" Blake let the unfinished sentence ride the quiet of the room.

"What are you saying?"

"Vince was good at hiding the truth," Blake said finally as he lifted her sweatshirt and carefully unwrapped the bandage around her torso.

"He saved Ethan's life."

"He put you both in danger." Blake laid the blood-stained gauze on the table between them and pierced her with an accusatory gaze.

The chill in the air no longer came from the winter

weather, but from his anger. Amanda looked up at him. "He did the best he could."

Blake's hot gaze flashed. "You want to know what your precious brother did? He wanted me to play their game. Look the other way. That's what I wouldn't agree to. That's why he framed me and hung me out to dry. Paul Irving in Internal Affairs tried to help. Even he couldn't stop them from railroading me."

"Vince wouldn't have."

Blake pulled out Betadine and more bandages from the Maddox house's medical kit and soaked some of the clean strips with the brown liquid. "Face it, your brother was involved with them, Amanda. That's why you were shot. That's why we're hiding out. Vince was a bad cop. He was never my friend. He used me. Worse, he let you and Ethan stay with him when he knew it was dangerous."

Amanda reeled back, shaking her head. "I won't believe that. He wouldn't put my son in danger." Vince had taken care of her. It couldn't be true. She rubbed her temple. "No. He was a good cop. Maybe he was undercover. Investigating them."

"You can delude yourself all you want, but it doesn't change the facts." Blake retrieved tape and scissors and set them next to the bandages on the table. He crossed his arms. "I need the truth. Did you know all along? Are you still covering for him?"

"The truth? That's easy. I'd do anything for Ethan." Amanda jumped up from the table, uncaring that her side could have burst into flames. "Don't do me any favors. I've got a plan," she lied.

"You've got men on your tail who have access to police systems. Exactly what is your plan?"

"I want him safe." She looked up at Blake and a wave of utter fatigue melted her bones.

"Not much of a plan. That's a goal."

She swayed and sank back into the chair as all her energy ran out of her. Blake's face grew blurry. He let out a sharp curse and came toward her. She shrank away, but he kept coming.

"I'm sorry," he said. He held her shoulders and cupped her cheek. "Vince is a sore spot for me, but I shouldn't have taken it out on you."

"He was my brother. I won't believe he betrayed his best friend. Or me." She sighed and dropped her chin to her chest. "I can't."

He knelt beside her and caught her gaze with his. "I admire your loyalty," he said as he shifted her shirt aside. "Hurting worse than ever, isn't it?"

She let him drop the subject. They'd never agree, and she understood why. Besides, she didn't want to fight anymore. She hurt, she was tired and she wanted to be safe.

"If we're going to bring these guys down, you need to be well and healed so your actions match your bravery."

Amanda gripped her fingertips and looked down. "I'm not brave."

He lifted her chin. "You faced me. And I'm damn scary." He quirked a smile. "Just ask the kids I stopped for joyriding last weekend."

His eyes twinkled and the gold flecks sparkled. For a brief moment she saw a hint of the Blake she'd known in Austin. The man with an easy laugh and smile, joking with Vince. His dry sense of humor had been one of the first things that had attracted her.

He'd lost some of that joy. Who wouldn't have? But the small inkling of playfulness made her heart flutter.

He bent his head and his fingers explored her wound. She sucked in a sharp breath.

"Sorry," he muttered as he probed the tender skin. "It looks better. Not as inflamed. Maybe we lucked out." He swiped the gash with Betadine.

"So," she panted, trying to distract herself from the pain, "where do you think Vince hid the file? Did he send you a package?"

"The only thing I got from Austin was my last paycheck."

She couldn't process his words. With each stroke, her side exploded in fiery stings of agony. She wanted to run outside naked to cool the hurt. She couldn't stop the small cry from escaping.

Immediately, he stopped and stared at her, naked emotions showed on his face. The sorrow, the regret. A small tick pulsed at his jaw. He wasn't completely in control.

He swallowed and quickly wrapped her torso, finally pressing the bandage tight. "You're done," he said, his voice husky. His fingers lingered against the binding, hovering over her bare skin. "I'm sorry I hurt you."

"Feels better." She shifted a bit. "Thank you. For more than this. For saving our lives."

He shook his head. "I underestimated how much they wanted you. I put you in danger by staying at my place too long. It won't happen again." He lifted his hand and stroked the side of her cheek. "I promise."

She leaned into him, wanting the comfort, wanting the reassurance of his strong presence, knowing he wouldn't let her down. His hands stroked her arms, and she looked into his eyes. They burned hot, the green fire leaping under his hooded gaze—a familiar spark that smoldered beneath the surface the more time they spent together.

Her entire being flooded with need. She couldn't look away, and the awareness flaring between them became palpable and undeniable.

"I shouldn't," he said as he bent down, his face hovering inches above her mouth. "You're hurt."

"I know. But I can." She lifted her lips and pressed them against his.

Without hesitation, without comment, he returned her kiss, gently, reverently.

Amanda closed her eyes and clutched his shirt, letting the warmth of his lips, the tenderness of his touch reignite more than her passion. He lit a fire in her soul, ignited hope in her heart.

She sighed. He raised his head, then carefully, he lifted her in his arms and carried her down the hall.

Amanda laid her head against his shoulder. His heartbeat thudded against her ear and quickened as she rested her hand against his chest.

Her own pulse accelerated in response. She was in trouble. Big trouble.

And for this one moment, she didn't care.

Chapter Five

Blake's body thrummed with urgency as Amanda nestled against his chest. His knees trembled, not from her insignificant weight but from how much he wanted her. Not that he could do anything about it. The redness around her injury worried him. He prayed that the disinfectant and antibiotics would handle the infection that threatened.

His concern didn't stop his mind from wandering to a place he shouldn't go, though. If she weren't hurt, she could wrap her legs tight around his waist. If they didn't have clothes between him, he could sink into her and lose himself in her passion. He wanted to throw her on the bed and take her. Let his lust carry him away, but he couldn't.

This was Amanda. She was hurt, afraid and vulnerable.

She needed him to be a cop, not a lover.

Someday, he would revel in every touch, and before he'd finished, he would know every inch of her. Right now, he needed to be a gentleman.

Slowly, making certain he didn't jostle her too much, he carried her to one of the bedrooms. She looked up at him with a sultry and trusting gaze, her blue eyes deep as a darkening Texas sky.

He gently placed her on the bed and leaned over her, his body hovering just above hers. He took a pillow and placed it under her head. She clasped his arm as he tried to straighten.

"You're killing me." His fingertip trailed down her cheek to her throat. "Destroying my resolve."

She didn't answer just pulled his head down to hers and parted her lips.

A groan rumbled in his chest. He let himself taste her, exploring the sweetness of her mouth, eliciting a strangled cry from her lips. Amanda clung to him, but he knew they both wanted what they couldn't have. Not until she'd healed.

He pulled back. "You need to rest." He pushed the curls from her forehead and let his thumb drift under the shadowed circles below her eyes that reminded him why he had to resist her.

"Stay with me," she said. "I don't want to be alone. Not right now."

"Can I trust you to behave yourself?" he teased with a smile, not certain he didn't see a hint of vixen behind the fatigue on her face.

"I promise to keep my hands to myself." She let out a small yawn. "I'm too tired to tempt you."

"Lying there is temptation enough," Blake said. He kicked off his boots, eased onto the bed and turned on his side. "Is this okay?"

She looked up at him. "Why didn't you ever ask me out? After that Christmas Eve party."

"Vince," Blake said. "Rule number one is don't sleep with your best friend's sister. And I knew if I ever got you alone exactly where it would lead. Into bed."

"You didn't expect this, did you?"

"I never thought I'd have you beside me." He placed

a hand lightly over her shirt where the bandage circled her chest. "I hate that it's in this situation."

"Can you help us, Blake? Can you find out who's after us?"

"I have some ideas. Friends I can trust."

"Not cops."

He wanted to wipe the frown lines from her forehead. "A bit more unconventional than that, but they'll help us put these murderers away."

"You followed the best friend rules. You followed the cop rules. I'm not very good at rules." She reached a hand to touch his face.

"Then maybe I can learn something." He kissed her nose and settled down beside her. "Try to rest. I don't imagine Ethan will stay occupied much longer."

Blake didn't know how long he watched the rise and fall of her chest, the slight parting of her lips or even the wince as she shifted closer to him. He loved that she turned to him even in sleep.

The house was quiet, and he needed to make another call. Surely Logan would be around by now. Just as he shifted to the side of the bed, a loud whinny sounded from outside.

Blake stilled, his senses on alert. The hair on the back of his neck stood at attention and he focused on the noise filtering from outside. It wasn't right.

No time to waste. Blake tugged on his boots. Very gently he touched Amanda's shoulder.

Her eyelids flew open. "What's wrong?"

"Something outside."

He grabbed his Glock from the nightstand. Her eyes widened and she struggled to her feet, following him into the kitchen. He slipped into his sheepskin coat that still smelled of Amanda and handed her the truck keys.

"If anything happens, get Ethan and go to the Triple C Ranch. It's right off the county road going toward Big Spring. About ninety minutes if you push it. Tell Logan Carmichael I sent you. He can help."

"You're scaring me."

He donned his Stetson. "I'm being cautious. It's probably nothing."

He exited through the back of the ranch house and moved toward the sound of the unsettled horses. They snorted and he could hear them racing around their pen.

A series of far-off barks made Blake's stomach clench. "Leo!"

The dog didn't come.

From out in the pasture the rumbling of a tractor roared. What the hell? He whirled around, then stopped and stared at the snow-patched terrain in horror. Hundreds of feet away, the small figure of Ethan flailed on the tractor, bouncing as the machine barreled across the frozen terrain. The thing had to be going at least thirty miles per hour.

Leo chased after him, keeping pace with the equipment.

Cursing the infamous "Billy" for teaching Ethan to start the thing, Blake scanned the yard. He could take the truck from behind the house, but getting to Ethan would require Amanda's help. She didn't have the strength. Not with her injury.

He glanced at Maddox's prized quarter horse, Ginger, who shifted restlessly in the corral, a fence away from their prized bull. The breed could run fast. At least faster than the tractor. Easier to maneuver than the truck. Although, despite everything, at this moment, he wished he had Sugar. That horse could really fly. Blake raced to Ginger and mounted her bareback.

With a flick of his boots, he set the horse to a strong gallop. He grasped the mane and leaned forward as they leaped the fence.

"Come on, girl. Catch up with him."

The tractor looked small. It had to be running at full speed. Urging the horse onward, slowly, they closed the distance. As Blake got closer, he watched Ethan turn around in the seat and wave, a big smile on his face.

Unbelievable. The kid had no idea of the danger he faced. With the ice, one sharp turn or bounce and the machine would roll over. Ethan could be maimed or crushed.

Blake's heart galloped against his chest. He refused to let Amanda go through what he'd experienced. He could still picture the cop coming up to him in the police station, his face solemn. "There's been an accident. I'm sorry, Blake. Your son didn't make it." Even the memory of the words made Blake's heart bleed.

"Ethan, hold on!"

Even as Blake yelled, he knew screaming was useless. Ethan would never hear him over the roar of the motor. He kicked the horse's flank, and she increased her speed. They were gaining.

The tractor hit a bump. Ethan bounced in the seat. He nearly fell off the side. His smile faded. Panicked he opened his mouth and shouted something. Blake's gut twisted. He could make out the words. "Help me!"

Leo leaped toward the boy, but the dog could barely keep up with the speeding tractor.

"Hold on, buddy." Blake bent forward close to the quarter horse's neck. "Come on, girl. Get me to him."

Ethan sank into the seat and grabbed hold of the edge. At least he hadn't fallen off. It could've been so much worse. The joyride was no longer a lark. If only he would keep his wits about him.

The horse's muscles shifted under Blake's thighs. He squeezed tight, urging the animal on. No saddle made the ride more dangerous, but he'd done his share of midnight capers across the Western plains. Still, as he chased the speeding machine, he considered his options. He might be better off jumping from the horse and onto the tractor, not risking slipping off the sweat-slickened horse's back when he reached for Ethan.

Blake scanned the ice-covered ground ahead of the tractor. His heart dropped. An irrigation ditch. No way the tractor would miss it.

No way Blake could stop the tractor in time.

"Come on, Ginger. Faster." He gripped her mane.

As if sensing his urgency, the horse quickened her gallop. Blake gauged the distance remaining. It was gonna be close. Soon, the rumbling of the tractor screamed in his ears. The horse didn't wince at the loud noises. Thank God. Sugar would've been a nightmare here. Blake guided the animal alongside the equipment while Leo veered off slightly, giving Ginger more room.

Ethan turned his head and stared at Blake, eyes wide with fear. He didn't know if the near fall had stunned the boy or if he saw the danger ahead.

He reached out one arm. "Grab on to me, Ethan!"

In a move Blake couldn't have repeated, he scooped the boy into an arm and, with all the strength he possessed, tugged at the horse's mane. "Whoa, girl."

The galloping animal pulled back and veered sharply to the left, stopping on the edge of the irrigation ditch. The tractor dived headfirst over the edge. The equipment tumbled onto its side with a loud thud and a hiss of steam.

Blake strengthened his grip, snagged Ethan up and sat him on the horse's back. Together they watched as the rumbling mechanical beast gasped and sputtered dying breaths.

"It's just like Billy's tractor," Ethan said as he gaped at the mass of metal. "But it's too big for me."

"Yeah," Blake said, letting out a loud sigh amid Leo's rabid barking. He steadied his horse, slid off the animal and grabbed Ethan. He sat the boy on the ground and then patted the horse's neck. "Good girl."

Leo whined and butted Ethan's hand. The boy patted the dog and stared up at the animal who'd saved his life. "Can I pet her?"

"In a minute." He took Ethan aside. "Stay here."

Blake scrambled into the gully and turned off the still-rumbling tractor. "I owe Maddox a big one," he muttered, before climbing out of the ditch. He saw his savings dwindling mightily once he settled the debt.

Ginger walked over to where Ethan stood and nudged his hand with her nose. He looked scared but fascinated by the big animal. Blake strode over to them, his heart racing, but he forced himself to remain calm. "You can pat her nose. She's a sweet one."

Ethan reached out a tentative hand and touched her gently. The horse snorted and he laughed. "She's breathing hard."

"She worked hard to save your life," Blake said. "So did Leo. You could've been hurt."

Ethan looked down at the ground and scuffed it with his tennis shoes. "I wanted to play."

Unbelievable. He'd forgotten how resilient kids could be. After everything Ethan had been through, Blake would've thought the kid wouldn't want any more adventures. He grabbed the horse's mane. "Get on. Your mom's going to be worried."

Ethan bit his lip. "Do you have to tell her?"

"No, but you do." Blake grabbed Ethan by the waist and settled him onto Ginger.

Blake mounted the horse behind Ethan and guided the boy's hand to her mane. "Hold her here, but don't pull tight. Leo, come."

Ethan gripped the long hair and bowed his head. "I don't want to tell Mommy. I don't want her to cry again."

When Ethan was steady, Blake clicked his tongue and squeezed Ginger's flank. She settled into a walk. "Does your mom cry a lot?"

"At night. All the time. She doesn't think I know, but I hear her. She's afraid she's not a good mommy." Ethan twisted around, his face fierce. "But she is. She's the best mommy ever."

Blake swallowed at the boy's protective attitude. The kid was loyal to the bone. Amanda had done a good job.

"She loves you."

As they closed in on the ranch house, Blake could see Amanda standing near the barn, her arms crossed, glaring at them.

"She also gets really mad sometimes," Ethan whispered. He looked up at Blake. "Are you sure I have to tell her?"

"What do you think?"

Ethan let out an aggrieved sigh. Blake stopped Ginger, slid off the horse and set Ethan down.

Amanda ran to him, knelt in front of her son and clasped his shoulders. "Haven't I told you never to leave without telling me?"

"I just wanted to play." Ethan stared at her defiantly.

She sank on her heels. "You know better than to get on a big piece of equipment by yourself. You scared me."

"I'm sorry, Mommy." He bowed his head.

"I love you, Ethan. Just tell me when you want to play next time. Okay?"

His eyes brightened. "Did you see me on the horse? Her name is Ginger. She saved my life."

Amanda looked over at Blake, her eyes warm with thanks. "I know exactly who saved you, honey. Introduce me to Ginger?"

Ethan grabbed her hand and took her over to the quarter horse. As he described their adventure, Blake couldn't help but notice the awareness in Amanda's eyes or the way she kept staring at him. His body hardened, and he knew one thing for certain: As soon as she was well, he'd finally know what it felt like to take Amanda, to have her, to bury himself inside her.

He also knew another hard and fast fact: next time, he wouldn't be a gentleman.

AMANDA TRIED TO FOCUS on Ethan's excited chattering, the dog glued to his side. Her heart warmed at his broad movements and his over-the top description of Blake and Ginger riding to his rescue. This was the boy she remembered. Somehow, in saving her son, Blake had unlocked the fear around Ethan's heart.

She glanced over at the man she'd been forced to rely on while he rubbed down Ginger and returned her to the corral. If Blake hadn't snatched Ethan from the tractor... Her heart skipped a beat at the thought. She'd almost lost him three times in the last three days. She wanted to wrap him in bubble wrap to protect him, but she knew she couldn't.

Only one man could help them.

Blake didn't hide the heat in his gaze, or the want in his eyes. She squirmed under the passion-filled look. Her pulse leaped, her body responded, as if she were calling to him, waiting for him. She crossed her hands over her breasts and pebbling nipples. She shot him an aggravated glare. His eyebrow shot up as he scanned her body, lingering on her chest, then moving down to her hips and legs.

Ethan tugged at her pants. "You aren't listening."

"I'm sorry, little man—"

A muffler backfire sounded from a distance. Ethan shouted out in fear, but instead of clinging to Amanda, he ran over to Blake and jumped into his arms.

"Get to the house," Blake snapped, his voice tense and urgent. He hugged Ethan tight and ran behind Amanda.

She shoved inside, and as soon as Blake raced through the door, closed it.

"Turn off the lights," Blake said as Ethan clung to him. "I don't want any sign we're here."

Amanda hurried around the room on one side, flipping switches while Blake took the other, still weighted down with Ethan.

Her heart ached. Her son's message couldn't be more clear. She couldn't protect him. Or save him. Blake could.

Just as she flipped the last light, she caught sight of the intruder through a gap in the curtains. A truck lumbered next to the barn—unbelievably, a vehicle older than the ancient one they'd used to escape.

Blake leaned over her shoulder. "The Collins kid," he said. "He takes care of Maddox's horses. If we stay quiet, he'll do his thing and move on. Get away from the front windows. I don't want to attract his attention."

With Ethan still clinging to him, Blake led her to a small, formal living room off the great room. Because it faced the back of the house, they were out of sight.

Blake knelt down, but Ethan just wrapped his arms tighter around Blake's neck. He sat on an oddly shaped sofa, looking much too big for the furniture, and planted Ethan on his lap.

"We're safe, buddy. That noise was just an old car."

Ethan peered up at Blake, his expression solemn. "Not a gun? You're not going to get dead like Uncle Vince?"

Amanda bit her lip to keep a cry from escaping. She started toward him, but Blake sent her a small shake of his head, and she paused.

"Where's your truck, buddy?"

Ethan stuck his thumb in his mouth. "In the tent."

Blake met Amanda's gaze, and she nodded. She didn't know what he was planning, but Ethan had started talking a bit about that night for the first time outside of his nightmares. She strode down the hall and after locating the truck headed back to the living room.

"I need your help, buddy," Blake said, his voice echoing from the formal living room. "Tell me what happened that night."

Amanda's breath caught as she hurried into the room. Ethan's frightened gaze flew to his mother's and he shook his head. "I can't talk about it."

"I need you to tell me, Ethan."

He shook his head back and forth. "I can't. I can't."

Amanda knelt beside the sofa and pulled Ethan into her arms. "That's enough," she hissed. "It's too much for him."

"We need to know," Blake said, his hand on her arm. "Until we do, we're sitting ducks."

"There's got to be another way," Amanda said.

She pushed the truck at Ethan to try to distract him, but he shoved it away and crawled off the couch to a small nook beneath an end table. He wrapped his arms around himself and rocked back and forth, muttering, "Don't talk. Be quiet."

He repeated the phrase over and over. Leo plopped down beside Ethan and whined, but even the dog couldn't offer her son any comfort. Amanda's heart ached for him. She scooted closer and gazed up at Blake. "Find another way," she repeated.

He shoved his hand through his hair as he stared at Ethan. "There's only one other option. I could go to Austin and search Vince's house."

Amanda reeled back on her heels. The idea of returning there… "We can't. It's too dangerous."

"*You're* not going anywhere. I know of a safe place you can stay. I'll go."

Half of her wanted to huddle with Ethan—protected and hidden—and to convince Blake to go with them, but his resolute expression was unbending.

"What if they're waiting for you?"

"I'm a cop, Amanda. I can handle myself. Besides, I have no choice. I have to go to Austin if you and Ethan want a chance at a normal life."

Amanda stroked her son's head, knowing what she had to do. "You can't search the entire house by yourself." She paused. "This place you want us to hide. It's really safe?"

"Logan's ranch is a fortress."

"You trust him."

"With my life."

"With Ethan?"

Blake nodded carefully. "What are you thinking, Amanda?"

She stood up and faced him, her own resolve strengthening. Now was the time to show her belief in Blake. To show Ethan his mother *would* protect him. "How long will the trip take?"

"If Logan loaned us a plane and pilot, we can be there and back in a half day."

Amanda took a deep breath. "Then I'm going with you. Now that I know Vince was hiding something, I can look for what's out of place. It'll take a lot less time than you on your own."

"It could be dangerous."

She shivered at the intensity of his gaze. "Any more than what we've already faced?"

Blake let out a long, slow sigh. "Probably not."

"Then I'm going. For Ethan's future. For the future Joey never had. Besides, you'll protect me. Right?"

"With my life." Blake grabbed his Glock. "Gather up everything. First thing tomorrow, we'll head to Austin and find that evidence."

Chapter Six

Early morning light slipped through the wooden slats of the Redmond barn. "That damn horse should be put down," Johnson muttered as he sidestepped the open stalls down the barn's aisle. He gave the one beast in the abandoned building a wide berth. "Last time, the thing almost killed me."

"Yeah. He came in handy, though," Detective Farraday chuckled. "Got rid of a suspicious witness, and drove Blake back to this Podunk town all in one shot."

Johnson shivered at the satisfied expression in the homicide cop's eyes. The man scared him. He didn't know how Farraday had passed the mental exam for the police department. He was one step removed from a psychopath. Maybe less than a step. Farraday liked hurting people. Liked watching them die. He and that horse should get a house together.

For a countless time in the last few days, Johnson's instincts fired another warning. He had to find a way out of this mess. The horse whinnied and pounded his hooves against the ground of his stall. If Johnson got out of this barn alive.

"I'm going through every inch of this hay-infested nightmare," Farraday said. "Be just like Blake to hide the evidence with this devil horse."

"If you don't want to get trampled, help me chase him into the corral. I don't know why he came back." Johnson cautiously moved toward the stallion's stall and shot Farraday an irritated glare. "I'm not going into that monster's den while he's there. That's suicide."

"Hang tough, coward." Farraday smiled at Johnson as he searched one of the adjoining stalls and let out a sharp curse. "Damn Blake and this cowtown. Just stepped in it. No file. No disk. No nothing." He slammed his hand against the wood. "We don't even know what we're looking for. Let's just torch the whole place. House, barn, everything." He scraped his fine leather shoe against the hay. "Sh—"

"Boss doesn't want to call attention. And he wants to be sure."

"He's gone soft."

"*You* tell him that."

Farraday exited the stall and limped across the barn. He slammed his fist on the tackbox. "Where the hell is it? The bitch *must* have met up with Blake because of the evidence." He rubbed his knee, then his bandaged left arm. "She's gonna pay. I can't wait to get at her."

The horse whinnied and darted toward Farraday. "But not before I kill that animal."

Farraday pulled out his Glock and aimed it at the horse's head. It snorted and slammed against the side of the barn, eyes wild. Johnson's heart pounded as he ducked out of the way of the crazed animal.

"Are you out of your mind? A bullet hole in a horse's brain will set off alarm bells."

"Tough. Locals will probably think Blake finally killed the horse for taking out his dad." The beast charged Farraday. "We're gonna kill them all anyway. I think that'll get noticed."

"Boss wants it done smart."

A rumbling sound broke through the argument. Johnson stilled. When the engine's purr grew louder, he cursed inside. Just what he needed when Farraday had the red eye. Maybe the vehicle had taken a wrong turn.

The car stopped. Figured. This entire situation had cratered. He should've taken his family and run when he had the chance. "Quiet. Someone's outside."

"Sheriff? You here?" A voice called out.

Johnson peeked around the doorway. Deputy's car. A young man climbed out of the vehicle and studied the area. Of all the luck. The damn horse pranced and rammed into the side of the barn.

The deputy snapped his head toward the building.

"Thanks a lot," Johnson muttered at the horse. He shot a sidelong glance at Farraday. He recognized the frenzied excitement. The deputy was toast, and he didn't even know it.

"Don't," Johnson protested, hoping to drag common sense back into his partner. "We should hide behind the barn until he leaves and finish the search.

Farraday smiled and pulled a batch of firecrackers out of his pocket. "We have a perfect weapon." He glanced at the stallion. "He did it for us once."

The deputy pushed open the barn door. "Sheriff Redmond? You here? Parris asked me to check the place out."

He walked in just enough, and Farraday shoved him toward the horse. The deputy stumbled to the center of the barn and whirled around.

"What the hell—" His voice trailed off as his eyes cleared in recognition. "The Austin cops."

"Sorry, kid," Farraday said.

He wasn't sorry, though. His eyes gleamed as he set off the firecrackers.

The horse raised up, wild-eyed. The deputy turned around and raised his hands. "No, Sugar. Calm down."

The horse stomped down on the deputy, slamming hooves against the man's head. He fell to the ground, unmoving.

Farraday opened the barn door and waved the panicked horse out. He picked up the pieces of the firecracker and shoved them in his pocket. "Worked like a charm the second time, too. Blake'll put the horse down this time for sure. He'll blame himself. Like it should be."

Johnson watched with shock as Farraday stepped over the kid's unmoving body, without a care or a hint of regret.

"Why do you hate Blake so much?"

Farraday looked up from the demon horse's stall, his gaze so ice-cold that Johnson shivered. "He put my name in front of IA. The investigation nearly cost me my pension. Did cost me my wife and kid. He's going to pay, and I'm gonna pull the trigger."

AFTER A SLEEPLESS NIGHT of dreams in which Amanda had her way with every inch of Blake's body and a suitably cold shower the next morning, he bundled Amanda, Ethan and Leo into the SUV from the Maddoxes' garage. In some ways Blake hated to leave. They were safe here; Amanda would have a chance to heal. Problem was, he had no telling how long it would last.

He could run, take them into hiding, but his gut churned at the idea of letting these guys get away with murder. He couldn't let that happen. For Joey. And for Ethan.

The Austin cops were still in his town. Everyone was at risk as long as they were here. No telling what they'd do. Parris could handle most anything, but he shouldn't have to. The perps hadn't just come to Carder because of Amanda. This showdown became inevitable the moment Blake had refused to go in with Vince. The moment Kathy and Joey had died.

The more Blake thought about it, the more he believed Amanda. His ex-wife and son had probably been murdered. His gut burned. The cops had blamed Kathy for losing control, but if she'd been anything it was overly cautious. He'd been too devastated at the time to question the investigators. Now, he wanted another look at those reports.

Blake scooted behind the steering wheel and shoved the keys into the ignition.

"I feel bad about taking your friend's car." Amanda pulled the seat belt across her lap and glanced in the backseat at Ethan and Leo, who never seemed to be more than a foot from each other.

"The guys who attacked my ranch know what we're driving. We can't afford to attract their attention. The SUV will blend in. The old truck doesn't, even in these parts," Blake said, tilting his Stetson back. "Besides, old man Maddox knows who it belongs to. He borrowed the rustbucket from my dad enough times."

"At least we have more room. You like Leo, don't you, little man?"

Ethan grinned and hugged the dog's neck. "I love him. He's my best friend."

"I know."

Amanda's face turned sad and solemn as Ethan snuggled close to the dog, then whispered to Leo, lost in his own world once more.

"He feels safe with the mutt," Blake said, his voice low. "He'll remember his old friends soon enough."

"That's just the thing. He didn't have any friends. We moved too much because of Carl's next big deal."

"Should I be looking over our shoulder for him?" Blake hadn't considered her ex until now. He didn't like the idea of another man touching her, holding her. Ever. But the man was Ethan's father. Blake would have tracked down Kathy across the country or the world if she'd taken Joey away. "Would he have followed you to see Ethan?"

She let out a cynical laugh. "If someone offered him money to find me, he'd be looking, but he'd screw it up. Probably get himself killed."

"He never sees Ethan?"

Amanda glanced into the backseat, and Blake took a quick look in the rearview mirror. Ethan was completely enthralled in a conversation with Leo.

"He promises. Never shows." Amanda's voice was a mere whisper. "I quit telling Ethan so he wouldn't be disappointed."

"And you weren't."

Amanda shrugged. "I don't matter."

"You're wrong." Blake turned onto a dirt road and rested his hand on her leg. Her muscles tensed under his caress, but he didn't pull away. He stroked her softly. "I dreamed of you last night."

She shivered, and he slid her a sidelong glance. Her eyes had gone dark again. She squirmed in her seat a bit as he eased his fingers down toward her knee, then back up her thigh. He wanted her used to his touch because he planned on exploring every inch of her. Soon.

She coughed and stilled his hand with her own. "Are you trying to make me crazy?"

"I'm distracting you, am I?" Blake smiled. "Just reminding you I haven't forgotten we have unfinished business."

Amanda glanced at Ethan. "Letting *things* go further is not a good idea."

"You've said that before, but that won't stop the inevitable." He let his fingertips slide inside her thigh, and a small whimper escaped her. "It's going to happen."

"Were you always this arrogant?"

She placed his hand back on the steering wheel. He let her. For now. He couldn't touch her the way he wanted with Ethan in the backseat. When he got her alone again, though… His body tensed in anticipation. He would take his time to uncover every erogenous zone she possessed.

He maneuvered the SUV onto a paved road and slowed down. The blacktop's shiny patches warned him of more black ice. "I hope folks stay inside today," he muttered.

As he changed lanes the car veered to the right. Blake kept his foot off the brake and turned into the gentle slide before he felt the wheels take traction. He straightened the car out and kept his speed slow.

"You should be helping the people in your town through this storm. I'm sorry you're stuck with us."

"Smithson will watch the roads. He's an up-and-comer. Parris will handle the rest. He could've been sheriff as easily as me. If not better. He knows the folks in Carder, and they look up to him."

"They wanted you."

"They felt bad about my dad's accident. Some of them still see me as the hell-raiser son of the 'real' Sheriff Redmond."

She raised a brow. "Seriously? You? Straight-and-narrow Blake Redmond?"

"I did my share of trying to prove I was cool even if I was the sheriff's kid. Once, I sat on the outskirts of town with a buddy drinking beer. We didn't drive, but we had alcohol in the backseat. I've never seen my dad so disappointed. My folks had to attend an alcohol awareness program with me. He was furious."

"They were there for you."

"Yeah. Tell that to my dad, the sheriff, who was supposed to be the one teaching the class. Made me pay for the guest lecturer they brought in from San Antonio." Blake let out a low whistle. "I'd been saving up for a Jet Ski. I never did get one."

"He loved you enough to help you do the right thing." She glanced behind her. "That's what I want for Ethan."

"I hated him at the time, but later I realized he was a great dad. We'd finally become friends."

Blake didn't know what his father would have thought about this situation.

Yeah, he did.

He would've protected Ethan with his life, but in the end, there were consequences for every action. Blake had to keep Amanda and Ethan alive long enough to do the right thing—and make sure the murderers paid for what they'd done.

She placed her hand on his leg. "I'm sorry."

"Me, too." He wanted to find a way to keep those consequences far away from Amanda and Ethan. The boy deserved not to be afraid. And he deserved the mother who loved him, who had sacrificed everything for him.

Blake couldn't resist touching her. He laced his fingers with hers and squeezed. Her fingers squeezed back, and Blake felt his heart ease.

Miles passed, but strangely, Blake didn't feel the need to chitchat. He couldn't remember the last time he'd been able to just be silent in the company of a woman. Amanda glanced at the landscape. He could practically see her mind whirling. Then she bit her lip and glanced once more back at her son.

"You're worried about going back to Austin."

"What if they catch us? What if I can't get back to him?" she said softly, her eyes never veering from Ethan as he whispered to Leo. "I promised myself I wouldn't leave him."

She was right to be afraid. If these guys were as well-connected as he believed, she'd end up one more border statistic, in a mass grave, one of hundreds of bodies never identified.

"You can stay," he offered.

"If there's a chance Ethan can have a normal life—" Amanda glanced at the road sign. "I thought you said Carmichael's place was toward Big Spring? We're going the wrong way."

"Not to throw the dogs off the scent." Blake pulled into an abandoned bar and retrieved his phone from his pocket. Quickly, he slipped the battery back in. "This can be tracked now."

She looked at the cell in alarm. "They know where we are, where we've been?"

"No. I'd removed the battery to the GPS. We were fine. Now, when I turn it on, it'll activate. If they're watching—and I'm certain they are—they'll head this way."

"You're using us as bait?"

"I won't sacrifice your safety." Blake removed her

hand from his leg. Suddenly, her touch felt wrong. "I'd have thought you'd recognize that by now."

"I'm all Ethan has. I have to protect him."

He recognized the stubborn thrust of her jaw, but he couldn't deny the twinge of hurt her assumption left on his heart.

"If we find enough evidence in Austin, he'll be safe."

"And if we don't?"

"You may not have faith in me, but you believe in your brother."

Slowly, she nodded her head. He couldn't believe she still trusted Vince after he'd put her in danger. Biting his tongue against a scathing retort his former best friend deserved, Blake exited the SUV and took the phone into the abandoned bar.

He powered on the cell and dialed a number.

"What the hell's going on Blake?" Logan Carmichael didn't mince words. "You call me, but won't leave a message. Parris shows up with your mother and won't say squat."

"I need your help. Below the radar. Can we get into your place unnoticed?"

"Come to the front entrance. I'll man the cameras. Pull to the back of the house," Logan said, as if he'd planned for the question. "And by the way, get out of sight of that old bar. You're like a beacon."

Logan was good. Blake ended the call, wiped the phone's memory and set it on the hardwood floor. The inch-thick layer of dust scattered. The wood had rotted, disintegrating in patches, much like Blake's entire world.

Amanda pulled him in divergent directions. She'd restarted his heart, but how the hell could he let himself get emotionally involved with her? She was trouble.

And in trouble. His heart could end up as hollow and crumbling as this old building.

He strode back to the SUV. "We're set. Ethan will be okay at the Triple C. Logan lives in a fortress. It's where Parris took my mom."

The news seemed to calm Amanda.

Blake restarted the car and pulled out on the road before taking the nearest all-dirt detour. "Back roads. Wouldn't want to meet our friends as they head toward that bar."

"You think like a criminal," she said, still staring out the window. "I might need lessons."

Blake reached for her hand and squeezed it. "Don't let yourself go there, Amanda. Once you do, it's hard to come back."

A haunted expression crossed his face. "I did some undercover time for the Narc unit before I made detective. No one should do that gig more than three to five years. It's easy to slide."

"Did you?"

"I wasn't in long enough. The assignment was the last straw in my marriage. I became a different person. Hours were crazy. I couldn't call her." He gripped the steering wheel and turned onto a dirt road. "She couldn't deal with not knowing where I was, what I was doing. She didn't trust me to be faithful...or not to get killed."

Blake shook off the memories as Ethan hummed in the backseat. "Point is, you don't want to live in fear. It changes you and impacts everyone around you."

"I may not have a choice."

It took another ninety minutes before he drove under a large iron arch adorned with a horseshoe and three Cs. He stopped at the locked fence and gazed into the cam-

era. He didn't have to say a word. The gate swung open.
Logan was as good as his word.

"Wouldn't want to try to break into this place," he
said. "Logan's set it up like a fortress. Nothing goes on
here that he doesn't know about."

They drove down a winding driveway and pulled behind a large ranch house, its back porch spanning the
entire dwelling. Logan Carmichael stepped out from
the door, the scar on his right cheek still an angry red.

"Can we trust him?" Amanda asked.

"I do. With my life." Blake stepped out of the SUV
and shook Logan's hand. He'd be stretching his friend-
ship to the max today.

"This had better be good." Logan's voice trailed off
when he caught sight of Amanda pulling Ethan from the
backseat. Leo jumped down and followed them around
the car.

"Later," Blake said.

He made the introductions, just as his mother ran
down the steps and flew into Blake's arms, a dollop of
flour smudged on her cheek.

"What's wrong, honey? Deputy Parris practically
dragged me out of the house and wouldn't tell me a
thing. Just dropped me here and took off again." Her
face blushed a bit and she shoved an errant strand of
cinnamon hair out of her eyes. "Didn't even give me
time to curl my hair."

"Sorry, Mom. It's been crazy." Blake squeezed her
tight and kissed her cheek. At least she was okay. Ever
since his dad had been killed he'd worried about watching out for her. It was the main reason he'd moved home.

"Logan treated me to a nice breakfast, but he won't
say a word. Not that he was ever the talkative one." Her

eyes widened as she caught sight of Amanda and Ethan. "And who is this strapping young man?"

Ethan shrank behind Amanda and peeked out from behind her.

His mother's sharp gaze caught sight of the yellow truck. She gave Blake a speculative glance and knelt in front of Ethan. "That's a nice truck you have."

Ethan held the toy close. "Sheriff Blake let me play with it. It was Joey's. He's in the clouds."

His mother blinked and she ruffled Ethan's hair. "Yes, he is. Well, Joey would be glad a little boy can play with his toy."

Blake cleared his throat. "Mom, do you think you could find Ethan something to eat?"

She smiled. "I can do better than that. Do you like chocolate chip cookies? I've been baking to keep busy. The little gal who runs the kitchen just took some fresh from the oven. They're about cool enough for a little boy to eat."

Ethan's eyes lit up. He glanced at Amanda. "Can I?"

Her smile trembled, but she nodded. "Sure, little man."

He grabbed his truck and walked beside Blake's mom, but didn't reach for her hand when she held it out to him. She looked down at him and frowned. Blake recognized the curious glance she threw over her shoulder. Oh boy, he'd have to answer more than a dozen questions before this thing played out.

Once Ethan was in the house, Blake turned on Logan. "Where's Parris?"

"He couldn't reach Smithson. Went to search for him. Then asked me to guard your mother until he could get back. What's going on, Blake?"

"I had some visitors this morning. Shot the hell out

of my house. I need to know Mom is safe while I get to the bottom of it."

"And I'm guessing this little lady and her boy have something to do with your trouble."

"Sharp as ever. I need to get to Austin. Check out something, but I can't take the boy. It's not safe for him. Physically or emotionally."

Logan crossed his arms. "You want me to babysit?"

"That kid's seen a man die. He's been shot at. He nearly died on a runaway tractor. He needs protection and supervision. Mom can do the cuddling."

"Maybe I shouldn't leave him alone after all." Amanda chewed on her lip, her hands kneading in front of her.

"Do you want to take him with us? Back into that house?"

She shook her head.

Blake shoved his hand through his hair. "I could leave you both here. Logan will keep you safe."

"I want to stay." Amanda sighed. "But I've got to *do* this. For Ethan. And for Vince."

Logan gave Amanda a sharp look, then turned to Blake. "Vince? Vince Hawthorne, that lying piece of—"

"Vince was murdered, Logan. Amanda is his sister."

He let out a low whistle. "I haven't heard anything about a downed cop."

"That's just one of our problems. And I'm not going into details. You have to trust me. And I need to get to Austin. Fast."

"Rich can take you in the Piper Lance. It'll get you there in an hour. And he'll watch your back."

"Good." Blake turned to Logan. "Can I use some of your men to back up Parris and Smithson? There are at least two guys in town. Maybe more. And I need a computer to get at some reports in the Austin PD databases."

Logan raised an eyebrow. "You really want to step in it, don't you?"

"Can you get me in?"

"Of course," Logan said with a wry smile. "Nothing I like better than bringing down dirty cops. You ready?"

"I need to say goodbye to Ethan," Amanda said.

Logan escorted them into the house. The scent of freshly baked chocolate chip cookies permeated everywhere. Amanda heard a soft voice singing and veered toward the sound. Blake's mother sat on a leather sofa, a glass of milk and a half-eaten cookie on the table next to her, a book in her hand. Ethan lay against her, his eyes closed, snoring softly.

"It'll be okay. I wouldn't let my mother stay here otherwise." Blake placed his hand on Amanda's shoulder. The vulnerability in her eyes made him hurt for her. She nodded quietly. He watched as unspoken communication went from his mother to Amanda. His mother nodded and she laid a protective hand on Ethan's back.

Amanda walked out of the room. Blake followed. "I want to be back soon," she said.

"Rich is prepping the Piper," Logan said. "You should be ready to take off in a few minutes."

Blake stuck out his hand. "We'll be back as soon as we can. If anyone comes asking…"

"I didn't see you."

Blake paused for a moment and met his friend's world-weary gaze. "Especially the cops."

"I'll evade the questions as long as I can," he said, his face determined. "You'd better take this." Logan handed him a cell phone. "It's traceable, but only by me and my men."

"Thanks. Give Parris and my mom the number. No one else."

Less than a half hour later, Blake and Amanda strapped into the Piper Lance.

"What if they're waiting for us?" Amanda said through the headphones.

"Logan set up a car so we can stay under the radar," he said. "We'll approach on foot. You've been gone two days. I would imagine they've searched the house. And if they'd found anything, they wouldn't still be after you."

She nodded, and Blake watched the tapping of her foot as the flatness of the West Texas skyline gave way to Austin's rolling hills and trees. Amazing what ninety minutes in a plane could do.

Blake had thought the first time he'd made the trek to Austin, he'd found home. He'd been wrong. It wasn't the place that made home, it was the people.

The plane landed.

"I need to check on Ethan," Amanda said quickly. "Please."

Blake powered on the phone Logan had given him, punched in a number and handed it to her. She placed it to her ear and closed her eyes in relief.

After a quick conversation with Ethan, she let out a sigh. "He's okay. I don't even think he misses me."

She returned the phone to Blake, and as her hand brushed his, a tingle of awareness fired through him. He gripped her fingers and squeezed.

She cleared her throat. "Parris wants to speak with you. He said it's important."

Blake didn't let go of her hand. "Parris? Did you locate the Austin cops?"

"We found Smithson in your barn. Sugar kicked him in the head. He's in a coma."

Chapter Seven

The plane eased up to the Austin-area fuel station near a half-full hangar, but Blake didn't budge as they came to a stop. Amanda could hear the strain in his voice and see the tightness around his mouth, the spasm in his jaw. As he bit out soft, yet staccato questions, she put the pieces together of what had happened to Blake's deputy. Her heart twisted in sympathy.

The same horse that had killed his father.

She couldn't imagine how he felt, but he didn't show it. With each passing second, the frown line between his eyes grew deeper. How long could he keep such a tight rein on his control without exploding?

"I shooed Sugar out of the barn. What would have possessed him to come back?" Blake rubbed the bridge of his nose. "Tell the vet what happened, but don't let anyone else deal with the situation. I'll take care of it when I get home. Just make sure you put the word out to the surrounding ranches that Sugar's dangerous. And keep me informed about Smithson. Tell his wife…" Blake paused. "Tell his wife I'll be by as soon as I can."

He ended the call. Amanda placed a hand on his arm, but he shrugged her away. "I should've told everyone to stay away from my place."

The plane's engines stopped. "Problem?" Rich re-

The Reader Service—Here's how it works:

If offer card is missing write to: The Reader Service, P.O. Box 1867, Buffalo, NY 14240-1867 or visit us at www.ReaderService.com.

NO POSTAGE
NECESSARY
IF MAILED
IN THE
UNITED STATES

BUSINESS REPLY MAIL

FIRST-CLASS MAIL   PERMIT NO. 717   BUFFALO, NY

POSTAGE WILL BE PAID BY ADDRESSEE

THE READER SERVICE

PO BOX 1867

BUFFALO NY 14240-9952

Play the Lucky Hearts Game

and get...
2 FREE BOOKS and
2 FREE MYSTERY GIFTS...
YOURS TO KEEP!

yes! I have scratched off the gold card.
Please send me my *2 FREE BOOKS* and
2 FREE MYSTERY GIFTS (gifts are worth about $10).
I understand that I am under no obligation to purchase
any books as explained on the back of this card.

Scratch Here!
Then look below to see what your
cards get you...2 Free Books
& 2 Free Mystery Gifts!

❏ I prefer the regular-print edition
182/382 HDL FS46

❏ I prefer the larger-print edition
199/399 HDL FS46

FIRST NAME

LAST NAME

ADDRESS

APT.#

CITY

Visit us online at
www.ReaderService.com

STATE/PROV.   ZIP/POSTAL CODE

Twenty-one gets you
2 FREE BOOKS and
2 FREE MYSTERY GIFTS!

Twenty gets you
2 FREE BOOKS!

Nineteen gets you
1 FREE BOOK!

TRY AGAIN!

© 2011 HARLEQUIN ENTERPRISES LIMITED. Printed in the U.S.A.

▼ DETACH AND MAIL CARD TODAY! ▼

HI-LH2-07/12

moved his earphones and shifted in the pilot's seat to look at them.

"Something I'll deal with. After we lock up these guys." Blake's lips thinned. "Keep the plane ready. We may have to leave quickly."

"Logan said to back you up," Rich argued.

"I need you standing by in a separate location. If this goes wrong, get word to Logan and fly Amanda out. Fast."

Rich studied Blake for a moment, then nodded. The pilot unlatched the plane door and pushed it open. Icy air blasted into the cabin, the cold biting her cheeks.

He helped her out of the Piper and indicated the private airport's terminal as Blake jumped down behind her. "I'll get the keys to the car. Stay out of sight."

Rich headed toward the building no larger than a double-wide. Amanda shivered as a wicked gust of wind slapped against her. She tugged at the edges of her flimsy coat. It was like she'd never left Austin. Yet so much had happened.

Blake reached into the airplane and pulled out a down jacket. He handed it to her. "Put this on. It's a gift."

She took the coat. The soft down beckoned her. She slipped her arms into the large jacket. She hated the idea of charity, but the weather had become too vicious to be anything but thankful. Before she could zip the coat, Blake brushed her hands away and quickly fastened the front. He fished a pair of gloves from the pockets and slipped them on her hands, lingering before he squeezed gently. "You can't afford to come down with pneumonia," he said, his voice husky.

She looked from the warm gloves to his reserved stare. Tension emanated from him, his expression carved in stone, set and intent, and yet he focused on her comfort and warmth, his actions tender and caring.

He tried to release her, but she refused to let his hands go. She held fast and looked up at him. "I'm sorry about your deputy."

His eyes blazed with self-loathing. "I knew the horse was one tantrum away from killing someone else. Who else can I blame but myself? My choices. My fault. At some point, you have to take responsibility for your actions. My dad taught me that."

"You're not responsible for everything that happens in Carder. You can't protect everyone."

"I'm the sheriff. They count on me." Blake pried his hands away from her grip, and Amanda's heart sank. He didn't want her comfort—or her touch. He'd retreated into himself. As gentle as he'd been with her, he closed himself off to those same needs.

He pulled out the Glock, double-checked the safety and gave her two clips from the inside of his sheepskin jacket. She recognized the need to control, especially when their world had spun into chaos. He handed the weapon to her. "I hope you won't need this, but I'm not taking any more chances with you."

She pocketed the weapon and bullets just as Rich crossed the airport toward the hangar.

He tossed Blake the car keys. "You're all set. Sedan's behind the hangar. Logan says be quick. Chatter seems to be picking up."

Blake's expression grew even grimmer. "We'll be in touch."

"I'll monitor the police frequency. If it goes south, I'll have your back."

"Thank you," Amanda said.

Rich gave her a small nod and disappeared into the hangar again.

"You ready?" Blake clutched the keys.

"I have to be, don't I?" Amanda shoved her hand in her pocket and encountered the gun metal, squeezing it. She'd used the pistol once since finding Vince. She prayed they would succeed and the entire nightmare would end before she had to use it again. "We'll find something, right?"

"I hope so." With his hand firmly pressed against the small of her back, he escorted her to the nondescript sedan and opened the passenger door for her. "What's the least obvious way to get into Vince's place?" he asked as he slid behind the steering wheel and turned on the engine.

"Back door. If you pull down the alley behind the house, we can go in the gate. I doubt anyone would see us."

Blake set the car into gear, exited the airport and pulled into traffic, navigating with ease. Amanda watched his hands as they held the steering wheel with a firm grip. Strangely, despite everything that had happened, she felt safe here with him. She knew he'd give his life to protect her...and Ethan.

Why couldn't he let her into his heart so readily?

"We're at least an hour away," he said. "Think back on every conversation you had with Vince. Did he mention a file or papers, discs or photos? Anything that would point us in the direction of the evidence our perps want."

"Nothing obvious. After you left town, Vince pushed me away. Would barely talk about anything. We didn't really visit much because our schedules were so different. A few emails. That was it." Amanda rubbed her temple. "I wish I'd asked. Maybe I would've known something. Maybe—"

"Vince had a choice, and he put you in danger."

She wanted to defend her brother, but she recognized the stubborn set of Blake's jaw. He was so like Vince, although she doubted Blake would appreciate the comparison.

"What kind of email?"

She blinked at his sharp change of subjects. "Email?"

"The emails he sent you? What were they about? Especially the last one. Try to remember as much as you can, Amanda." Blake glanced at her, his voice urgent.

"Most were just chitchat. A few jokes like the old Vince would've sent. Except—" She paused as a flood of insight washed through her. Oh, God. She'd forgotten until now. "He updated his beneficiaries." Her words were hushed. "Right after Kathy and Joey's funeral."

The words settled in the truck like a heavy blanket of foreboding. Every argument Blake had made raced through her mind. She wished doubts of Vince weren't creeping in, but she couldn't stop them.

Still, he'd had reasons for everything he did, even if he'd been impulsive. She twisted toward Blake. "Vince sent us to you. Are you sure he didn't send *you* anything?"

"Not after our last…altercation." Blake gripped the steering wheel, his knuckles white.

"You mean fight."

"My dad had just been killed, and I decided to give Vince one last chance. He'd been my partner, but I was out of time. Irving couldn't protect me any longer. The rest of IA was out for blood. Besides, no way could I stay in town and investigate with what my mom was going through." Blake vibrated with annoyance. "He ignored me. Just told me to leave it alone. Go back to Carder. Nothing I could do."

"Vince pushed you away. To keep you safe," Amanda argued. She could see the truth so clearly. Why couldn't he? "Just like he did for me."

"He was protecting himself," Blake said firmly. "I left. There was nothing in Austin to hold me, except nailing the traitors who framed me. My mom needed me. The town wanted me. And as Sheriff I'd have more resources I could trust to ferret out the truth."

Amanda fell back against her seat. "You've been investigating Vince since you left. Did he know?"

Blake shrugged as if it didn't matter. "He deposited money that couldn't be accounted for. He opened a separate account in another bank, in another town. I was close."

"You could have talked to him, asked him what was going on."

"Why would I confide in the man who forged my name in the evidence room when a stash of guns went missing? Besides, I had to be careful. They'd made me look more than guilty. I'm shocked they didn't throw me in jail. With the right prosecutor and judge, they would've been able to make it stick."

"Then why aren't you behind bars?"

"I've asked myself that same question more than once."

He turned down a quiet street, clearly wanting to stay off some of the main thoroughfares.

"You didn't go quietly."

"Hell, no. I was meeting with IA the morning—" His voice trailed off. "The morning my family died." Blake's knuckles went white on the steering wheel. "Damn them. They timed the accident that way. They killed Kathy and Joey to distract me, stop my questions."

Amanda shuddered, her mind whirling at the danger they faced. "They were innocent. Just like Ethan."

"Their plan succeeded." Blake's voice had gone low and cold, his fury punctuated in the bite of each word. "I was torn up. I let the investigation go. By the time I was myself again…they'd covered their tracks.

"Then Dad died. I left, but I knew Vince would tip his hand sooner or later. He could never bluff in poker either. Not for the entire game." Blake flicked on his blinker and eased the SUV into an exit lane. "Vince should've stood with me."

"I think he did. In his own way." Her idiot brother. Trying to protect everyone else. Never telling anyone what was going on. She gripped the denim of her jeans and worried the fabric. "What if *you* thought Vince was in real danger? What would you do?"

"Whatever it took."

"Vince was the same way, wasn't he?"

Blake didn't pause. "He was bullheaded. He'd grab hold of something like a rottweiler. Never let it go."

"And if you'd been convinced his family—me and Ethan—were in danger?"

"I'd have tried to get him out of the way while I…" Blake's voice trailed off. He shook his head. "Same logic works if I was hip-deep in corruption. Get the guy out of town who could bring me down."

"I can't believe you're calling *Vince* stubborn. Have you looked in the mirror? Everything is black and white with you, Blake."

"It has to be. Without certainty in right and wrong, it's too easy to take the wrong path. My dad taught me that, too."

"Then why aren't you turning me in for stealing that car?"

"Because right and the law don't seem to go hand and hand these days." Blake turned the corner and closed in on Vince's street. "The alley behind the house?"

"Yes. Turn on the next block."

Blake ignored Amanda and drove toward the front door.

"Are you crazy? Someone might see us," she hissed.

"Get down," he said, removing his Stetson. Her head rested on his thigh, and he slowly drove past the front door of Vince's house. "No crime scene tape. No cars. Place *looks* deserted."

He rounded the corner, then eased the car into a tight alley. "You can get up now." He pulled to a stop. "I don't like it. No way out if they block us in," he said.

"No one knows we're here."

"You assume. That's a sure way to get us killed." He faced her. "Vince's house isn't that big. The place has probably been turned already. But Vince wasn't a fool. He would've hidden the evidence out of sight. We should start in your or Ethan's rooms. He'd want you to be able to find it."

"So we're looking for a folder?"

"Could be paper, but more likely a CD or memory card. Anything that might have information on it. He could've hidden it anywhere. Focus on things you or Ethan would've taken with you. Backs of pictures, toys, valuables. If I were keeping evidence, I'd have stashed it in a couple of places. For backup."

"Like at a lawyer's?"

"Or in a safety deposit box." He unclicked his seat belt and turned to her. "Look for a key, too. Grab his address book if you can."

Blake put the vehicle in park and glanced around the quiet alley. "I don't like it, but better leaving it here than on the street to attract even more attention."

She reached for the door, but he placed his hand over her arm. "Wait."

He stepped out of the car and looked around, then motioned for her to follow. She exited the vehicle and stood by his side, staring at the six-foot cinder-block wall. She couldn't believe she was actually breaking in to her own brother's house.

She started toward the gate, but he held her back. "Too obvious. They may have it wired. We go over the wall."

Blake hoisted himself up with ease. He scanned the backyard for at least a minute through the branches of a large tree. "Looks clear." He dropped to the ground and cupped his hands. Amanda stepped into his grip, and in one quick movement she grasped the wall with her arms, ignoring the twinge on her side. She hooked her leg over and maneuvered to the top.

She'd never viewed the backyard from this angle. Ethan's baseball and bat lay in the lawn. His glove should've been nearby. She'd begged Vince to play outside with Ethan more often. She sighed. She understood now why he hadn't.

Blake's admonishments filtered through her mind. Why hadn't Vince sent them away? Why had he kept them close?

She knew the answer. All too well. He hadn't wanted to be just like their parents. There, but not there.

She shifted, getting ready to drop to the ground.

"Wait for me," Blake called.

He vaulted onto the wall and sat beside her. "We take

this slow and easy. We'll have to break in, unless you have a key. Is there an alarm?"

"It wasn't armed when I left. And there's a key under the planter. Vince stowed it there when I locked myself out one night after a late shift."

"One less thing to worry about."

He jumped down to the yard, his boots sinking into the ice-covered grass, turned and held his arms up to Amanda. She slid down the rough cinder-block, sliding down his body, her breasts pressing against his chest. Her breath caught and she looked into his eyes. They warmed slightly before the heat melted away. He set her aside.

"Just because we haven't seen anyone doesn't mean they're not checking out the place. I'm going in first. Don't follow until I motion to you. If something happens, get back to the plane. Logan will help you and Ethan disappear."

Blake pulled out his weapon. Amanda tensed as he ran across the lawn, half expecting a gunshot to come from nowhere. Once he'd navigated the backyard, he retrieved the key, unlocked the door, and after a few cautious seconds disappeared inside.

Her heart beat fast, worry for Blake contracting every muscle. She didn't know how long she waited. Every second felt like an hour. She shivered and rubbed her arms as the cold seeped in. The sun wasn't as intense here, and the coat didn't keep out the cold. Where was he? Had someone been in the house? What if something had happened to him? They never should've come here. Never should've tried to fight the inevitable.

Suddenly, Blake's broad shoulders stepped onto the patio. He raced back to her. "Come with me," he said.

He placed himself between her and the side of the

wall unprotected by trees and held out his hand. She grasped him, his touch warming her from the inside. Together, they raced to the house and plunged inside.

She gasped at the mess. The kitchen had been ransacked. Plates broken. Every container upended. Every cupboard open.

"Why?"

"They don't know what they're looking for, either," Blake said.

"They trashed the entire house? Even Ethan's room?"

"Not much to salvage. I'm sorry."

Blake rubbed her back in comfort, even as her heart broke. Not a drawer left untouched.

"It'll take too long to find anything," she said softly. "We won't have room to take much anyway."

"After we nail these guys, you'll have time."

Blake crossed his arms, his stance positive and unwavering. She couldn't help but admire his confidence, standing in the midst of a battle scene. She didn't see the hope. She saw destruction and anger that she had to protect Ethan from.

"So, they pretty much rifled through the obvious. If they'd found it, I don't think they'd ever have come to Carder."

"Unless they found something pointing to you," Amanda said.

"Good thought. Except Vince didn't send me anything." Blake paused and scratched his chin. "So now, we search the unobvious."

Amanda stepped from the kitchen into the dining room and couldn't keep the dismayed gasp from escaping. The few things she'd been able to keep of her mother's—a tea set, a picture frame, a small wooden box of keepsakes—were all smashed on the floor.

She clutched at her chest. She couldn't bring up one memory of her and her mother together, but Amanda had always dreamed. One day, she'd have had a place where that tea set, that picture frame would be safe, secure, at home.

"Gone. It's all gone."

Her emotions overwhelmed, she turned away from the destruction, only to land in Blake's arms. He wrapped her tight and stroked the back of her head. He said nothing, but the hard muscles of his chest, the strength of his arms comforted her. She wouldn't let herself cry. She couldn't afford the indulgence of emotions. She pushed him away.

"I'm fine." She walked past Vince's office, where she'd found him, and paused, her body tensing, afraid to see the empty shell that was her brother yet again.

She took a deep breath and stepped across the threshold.

"He's not there," Blake said. "No blood that I could see. They may have left traces, but they cleaned up."

"Vince wouldn't have left anything in his office," she said. "He hardly ever went in there."

"Where did he spend most of his time?"

"With Ethan. If he got home early enough, he'd tell Ethan stories. Ethan would smile and say they talked about guy stuff."

"Then we try Ethan's room."

They trudged up the stairs and pushed open his room. The destruction was less. Even some of Ethan's toys were untouched.

"Odd," Blake said.

"I'm just thankful," Amanda countered. She walked in and sat on the bed. "Maybe I can find a toy or two so Ethan won't be so—"

Her voice trailed off, and she sniffed in the air. "Do you smell something?"

Blake paused. They looked at each other.

"Gas." He grabbed Amanda's hand. "We've got to get out of here."

They ran down the stairway. The moment they hit the first floor, the odor became overwhelming.

"Not the kitchen," Blake choked.

They raced out the front door. Cold, fresh air slapped Amanda's face. She bent over, dizzy, sucking in deep breaths.

"Freeze!"

Blake straightened. A man in a cop's uniform faced them, his gun drawn, his face tense. Blake stepped in front of Amanda. "Glenn?"

The man lowered his weapon slightly, then raised it. "Blake Redmond? What are you doing here?"

A loud boom rocked Amanda on her feet. A blast of hot air hit and knocked her to her knees.

FIERY DEBRIS POUNDED across Blake's back. He stumbled forward. With horror, he watched a burning projectile hit Amanda on her shoulder. She dropped down.

"Amanda!"

He covered her with his body as raining fire pummeled him. He chanced a glance at what was left of Vince's house. If there'd been any evidence in there, it was gone.

Glenn stumbled to his feet, his face streaked with black. "Vince!" he cried and ran toward the house. Blake grabbed the man. "Vince's body isn't inside, man."

"He was scheduled to work today, then I heard the call come in from a neighbor about prowlers..." Glenn's voice trailed off, his gaze suspicious. "Body? What are you talking about?"

"Sorry, I can't talk about it. Not yet."

Glenn reached for his cuffs. "Then I'm taking you in. You and your girlfriend."

Amanda groaned and rolled to her feet. "It's me, Glenn." She coughed, as black smoke rose from the burning embers behind them. Her eyes streamed. "Blake's telling the truth. Vince is dead." She grabbed Glenn's arm. "Please, just let us go."

A movement caught Blake's eye. He glimpsed a man in a hoodie running from the alley.

Blake looked at Glenn. "Sorry, bud, I'll explain later." He slugged the man beneath the jaw, and Glenn sank to the ground, out cold. Blake took off after the suspect, but a car peeled out. Blake slowed down and cursed. He turned around and stared at Amanda, kneeling next to the cop who was a good guy but in the wrong place at the wrong time.

Sirens sounded from nearby. He rushed back to Amanda and grabbed her hand. "Fire department's coming. Glenn will be fine. We won't. We've got to get out of here."

Amanda stumbled behind him, and Blake cursed Vince once more. What had he been up to? And if he'd turned on the bad guys, why hadn't he come to Blake and brought him the evidence?

He skidded to a halt as they approached the car and held out his arm to block Amanda from getting too near. "Don't go any closer. Whoever set that explosion knew we were in Vince's house and was in the alley. The guy could've rigged the car."

"How did they know we were in Austin at all?"

Amanda panted. "Did Logan or his men give us away? Is Ethan safe?"

Blake lowered himself to the ground and searched under the car, looking for an explosive device or even a GPS. "Logan's pickier about the folks who work for him than the FBI. I trust him. My guess is whoever's the ringleader in this is monitoring activity. When the prowler call came in, they just piggybacked on the call. They saw us and decided to get rid of the witnesses and the evidence at the same time."

"But Ethan wasn't here. And he's their eyewitness."

"They might not know Ethan wasn't with us. Hell, if Glenn hadn't shown up, they might've tried to take us out. They want our deaths to look like an accident."

Blake didn't see anything unusual underneath the car. He slid from beneath the vehicle and stood up. "We have a problem, though."

"Can it get worse?"

"I'm afraid so. They were willing to blow us and the evidence up. If they've given up finding whatever Vince had, then they'll step up their game."

"Oh, God. They'll keep coming," Amanda muttered. "There's no choice left."

Blake cracked open the door and checked for wires, then popped the hood. Nothing. He spent enough time tinkering with cars, he'd recognize a faulty wire. The guy hadn't had enough time to do anything more sophisticated.

The sirens grew louder. No time left. "Stand back," Blake said. He slipped into the car and turned the key. The car started with ease. No hesitation. He gunned the engine, then pressed on the brakes. "We're safe. Get in," he said to Amanda.

She hesitated. Blake didn't blame her, but the sirens were nearly on top of them.

"We can walk," he said quietly. "Take the back roads and I'll contact Rich to pick us up."

A fire engine streaked past them.

"You're sure it's safe?" she said.

"I'll get you back to Ethan." Blake opened the passenger side and she slid in beside him. "We get on the plane, hightail it to Logan's ranch and regroup."

Blake sent her a sidelong glance. "Because now, you're not the only one on the run. The law's after me, too."

Chapter Eight

More sirens screamed closer and closer. They were coming for them. Blake had slugged a cop. Glenn knew Blake...him *and* Amanda. He gripped the steering wheel. He didn't like their precarious position in the alley. They had two options. Forward or back. If the Austin PD blocked both exits, they were caught.

A police car whizzed past them.

"Duck!" he snapped.

Amanda hunkered down, her head near his leg, her shallow, quick breaths revealing her fear. He let his hand touch her wild auburn hair, twirling the locks on his finger, hoping his touch would calm her. All the while his foot hovered over the accelerator, his entire body ready to slam the car into gear.

Flashing lights sped by, followed by a fire engine, ambulance and rescue unit.

They didn't slow.

Blake waited another thirty seconds before letting out a slow stream of air. "They passed us by."

Amanda pushed herself up. "I never should have involved you. If they catch us..." Her voice trailed off. "Ethan will be alone."

"I'm not letting that happen." Blake turned to Amanda. "I promised I'd get you back to your son, and

I will." He eased the vehicle forward to the end of the alley. With a quick glance, he saw the convergence of emergency equipment. "They'll be busy with the fire for a while."

He turned the opposite direction onto the street, his thoughts clicking through what he'd seen—and what he hadn't seen in the house. "This is going to sound strange, but are you sure Vince is dead?"

She let out a choked gasp. "His eyes stared straight through me. Blood was everywhere. He had a hole where his heart should have been. He was dead." Her voice shook with sorrow and more than a hint of betrayal.

"Okay, okay, I'm sorry." Blake rubbed her leg with his hand. "It just doesn't make sense. Why take the body? They could've used it to frame you and bring you in." He drummed his fingers on the steering wheel. "They didn't expect Vince to betray them," he muttered. "This was all a giant screwup. They're covering their tracks." Blake cursed. "And I let it slip to Glenn that Vince was dead. He'll ask questions. He may be in danger and not even know it."

Blake hit Logan's number on his phone. "This is Blake. We got trouble."

"Really?" Logan's sarcasm rang through Blake's ear. "I'm tracking the Austin police radio traffic. What have you done?"

"Among other things, put a good cop in danger. Glenn Romero. If he starts asking questions, I don't doubt they'll frame him like they did me."

"Get back here before they check the private airports. I'll keep an eye on the Romero situation." The sound of papers ruffled through the phone. "Think long and hard about how you want to play this. You're getting close to a no-win scenario."

"Losing isn't an option, Logan." Blake ended the call and glanced at Amanda. "It's not just you and me now. We've dragged in someone else. We have to find what Vince had on these guys another way."

She didn't respond, and he didn't like her silence. Her hair covered her face, and she twisted one curl around and around her finger. He'd let her down, but a wave of apprehension rose in his gut. "You're thinking too much. It's going to be fine. I'll figure out a way."

"How? Vince is dead. His house is in ashes. Any evidence he left is gone."

She gazed out the car window, shaking her head. Blake rested his hand on her shoulder. She didn't pull away, but he could feel the stiffness in her body. "Don't close me out," he growled. "I won't let them get away with this. I promise."

"Vince didn't have time to do anything with the evidence," she said, her voice flat and certain. "He never did plan ahead. You said so yourself. There's nothing left. We might as well accept it."

Blake didn't like the defeat in her voice. "We don't need Vince's files. I'll go back to my place. There'll be something to identify the guys who attacked my family's ranch. Ballistics, tire tracks, something. They've tipped their hand by coming after you and Ethan. That was a mistake. A big one."

"Maybe, but all I can think about is protecting Ethan."

"Amanda, don't give up. Now that we know how far they're willing to go, we can't give up."

Her utter stillness swelled his sense of unease. She nodded slightly, but he couldn't shake the foreboding.

She hadn't caught a lot of breaks in her life. He knew from what Vince had told him over the years she'd had few reasons to believe in anyone or anything. This time, though, she had an ally. Blake wouldn't stop until she and Ethan were safe, and Joey was avenged.

He wouldn't let her down, but he had some thinking to do. With a few turns, he took the quickest back-road route to the private airport outside of Austin and strategized. He was starting from scratch, and after this fiasco, he didn't have much time before he landed behind bars…or dead.

THE SUN SHONE THROUGH the windows, heating the inside of the small plane as it taxied to the Carmichael ranch's private airport. The bright rays should have warmed Amanda, but her soul had chilled. She wrapped her arms around her body, unable to stop the dark cloud that threatened to overwhelm her.

The fire had changed everything. For a few short hours, Blake had rekindled her hope for a normal life with Ethan. Now that was gone. Everything was gone. From the evidence to save Ethan to the antique teapot her mother had left her.

She'd run out of options.

She'd shut Blake out the entire trip, feigning sleep. In truth, she'd needed time to think. To plan. Blake wouldn't like her choices, but he would have to understand. Everything she did, she did for Ethan.

Once the plane pulled to a stop, Rich tugged off his headset and twisted in the seat. "Sorry it didn't work out."

Amanda stirred in her seat, pretending to wake up. She nodded but didn't comment. What could she say?

Blake's expression tensed as he studied her. "You feeling okay? Your side giving you trouble?"

She forced herself to meet his concerned gaze. It would have been an easy excuse, but then he'd want to look at it again, and she didn't want him touching her in tenderness. She couldn't afford to allow herself to count on him. "I'm fine. Disappointed," she said quietly. "Worried."

It was the truth. She would never get away with flat-out lying to him. Those intelligent, cowboy eyes saw too much.

He clasped her hand in his. "I'll protect you."

She didn't move so as not to alert his suspicions, even though she wanted to avoid his comforting touch. She had to rely on her own strength and be tough as a West Texas drought to keep her and Ethan alive.

The plane taxied to a stop just outside a hangar. "Logan's on his way," Rich said, "to take you back to the main house."

He helped Amanda out of the Piper. Blake followed. The frigid air stung her cheeks, but no more than the reality of her inevitable decision.

An SUV screeched to a halt. She and Blake hurried to the vehicle. Amanda pulled her hand from his and quickly slipped into the backseat. Blake gave her a speculative look before climbing into the front. Stupid. She had to keep cool. Blake was too smart and too perceptive.

"What's the latest?" Blake asked Logan.

"The Austin police tracked your original flight plan back to the Triple C. I put them off, but they'll be coming to search for you. Soon."

Blake let out a harsh curse. "Sorry to put you in this position, Logan."

"I'll survive. I've been through worse." A haunted expression darkened his gaze.

Amanda couldn't guess how Logan had injured his right cheek, but it must've been bad. The words made her more certain than ever she'd made the right choice. She couldn't let Blake sacrifice any more than he already had. Logan didn't need the trouble, either. The best thing for everyone would be for her and Ethan to get out of their lives.

She could do this.

As Logan pulled up to the house, Amanda steadied her nerves.

"We don't have long," he cautioned.

Blake turned to her. "Get Ethan ready. Logan and I have plans to make. We'll head out as soon as you're ready."

She nodded, fully aware that any other time she would've blistered him with words for being so high-handed as to plan her and Ethan's life. She would've peppered him with questions, pressed him to be involved. Not now. It didn't matter. She'd make her own plans.

"Amanda?" Blake's intent gaze willed her to look at him. "Do you trust me?"

"More than anyone else," she said quietly, and turned to Logan. "Where's Ethan?"

"In the house," Logan said. "He's attached himself to Blake's mama pretty tight."

As she walked away, Blake lowered his voice, speaking to Logan in a soft but urgent tone, his entire body taut with purpose. Part of her longed to run into his arms and spill out her fears, her doubts, but she couldn't let herself lean on him. He was brave, intuitive and determined, everything she wanted and needed. Nothing she could have.

Amanda climbed the steps to the ranch house, her legs weary, her very essence tired. The unexpected sound of Ethan's laughter bubbled up from the kitchen. Pasting a smile on her face, she followed her son's voice, although her heart remained heavy with trepidation. It had been so long since she'd heard that sound. It was unfair to bury it under more fear.

The warm kitchen had become a mass of ingredients and measuring spoons. Ethan had his arms elbow-deep in cookie dough and looked up adoringly at Nancy Redmond. Leo lay just outside the kitchen, watching Ethan with sharp eyes. Deputy Parris stood very close to Blake's mother while they watched over Ethan. Amanda's smile turned genuine at the picture.

Parris lifted his gaze and stepped quickly away from Nancy. His cheeks reddened. Interesting. Did Blake know?

"Didn't go well, I heard," Parris said.

"That's an understatement."

Ethan lifted his gaze from the cookie dough. "Mommy!"

"I'd better talk to Blake." Parris left the kitchen, his footsteps disappearing down the hall.

Her son shoved back from his chair leaving blobs of cookie dough in his wake. He launched at her. "Miss Nancy and me are making cookies. Peanut butter."

"Sounds delicious." She laughed. "How about you wash your hands and I'll get your face." She took him to the sink and lifted him so he could wash up. "You have fun, little man?" She kissed his forehead and hugged him tight.

"I like making cookies." The grin he gave her

warmed her heart. He looked like her son again, with joy in his eyes, without the burdens he carried.

She hoped he'd forget in time.

"Well," she said, rubbing his small hands between hers, "I think you like eating them more."

He grinned and nodded.

Nancy picked up two cookies from the cooling rack. "Ethan, can you take this cookie to Deputy Parris? He loves my cookies."

Ethan cradled the napkin in both hands. "But there are two."

"One is for my assistant."

Her son's eyes brightened. "That's me."

Nancy laughed. "Yes, that's you. Now skedaddle while I show your mama the secret to amazing peanut butter cookies."

Ethan took a quick bite. "It's the chunky peanut butter," he said, his mouth stuffed.

"Yes, it is." Nancy ruffled his hair. "Now go find the deputy."

Ethan shot out of the kitchen and Leo took off behind him. Nancy turned to Amanda. "What's going on? And don't try to shove me aside. Parris won't tell me anything, but I know something's very wrong."

Amanda squirmed under the woman's intelligent gaze. "Thank you for what you did for Ethan. I haven't seen him smile in too long."

"He's a good boy, but don't think that'll get you off the hook, young lady." Nancy folded a dish towel and set it on the sink. "I haven't seen Blake this intense in a long time. I'm not sure I like it."

Blake rushed into the kitchen carrying a sobbing Ethan plastered to him, Leo at his heels. "We've got company at Logan's gate. We're out of time," he said sharply.

"I'm sorry," Amanda said. "So sorry I brought this horror with me."

Nancy rushed across to Blake and grasped his arm. "Tell me what's going on."

Blake's face softened and he touched his mother's cheek. "Parris will fill you in. I'll be in touch, I promise. But I have to do this. For Joey."

Blake rubbed Ethan's back. The boy's sobs quieted a bit. Amanda tried to take him, but he clung to Blake's neck. She understood, even though it stung that her son turned to Blake.

Nancy's eyes widened, then looked between him and Amanda. She swallowed at the utter anguish on Blake's mother's face, and there was nothing she could do about it. Logan rushed in and tossed Blake a set of keys. "Vehicle's out back. It won't lead to me or Carder. Money's in the glove box. Take the side gate." He paused. "I hope to see you again."

"You're not coming back?" Blake's mother's eyes teared.

Amanda heart twisted. She grabbed Blake's arm. "Give me the keys. Let us go. I'm ready to disappear."

"Joey and Kathy's murderers are not going to win." Blake's harsh features stood out sharp as his mother gasped in shock. "I won't stop until I find them, *and* you and Ethan are safe. There are no halfways."

The scream of sirens penetrated from outside. Amanda's heart raced in panic. Blake grabbed Amanda's hand and dragged her through the kitchen door to the SUV. "Backseat. Hold Ethan," he said.

Shouts raged at the front of the house. Logan's fierce protests rose above the yelling. Stalling for time.

Amanda dived into the car and held her arms out. Blake lifted Ethan toward her, and her son scrambled into her arms. He didn't say anything, just pressed his head against her chest and hugged her tight. Leo jumped up and planted himself just beneath Ethan's feet. She stroked her son's hair and braced herself as Blake slammed the door shut. He got in, and once he started the SUV, floored it. Within seconds they were over a small hill and out of sight of the ranch.

She kissed the top of Ethan's head and turned around, studying the hill for any sign of flashing lights.

No one followed.

She sagged back against the leather and cuddled Ethan against her as Blake followed the barely visible road to a side gate. He stopped the vehicle to open it.

She met Blake's gaze in the rearview mirror and recognized the unwavering determination. Just like she thought. He'd fight for them, and as much as she wanted to accept his help, how could she let him sacrifice his life for them? His mother shouldn't have to lose her son. She'd never met a man so willing to put aside his own needs for someone else.

Blake took a hard right at the next county road. "We stay off the highways," he muttered. "Keep to the dirt, not the pavement."

The sun had nearly set by the time Blake turned into the Maddox place. He'd had to pull off as another screaming siren headed toward the Triple C. Now he slowed to a crawl.

She didn't see anything out of place.

He pulled in behind the house. "Wait here," he said. Within moments he was back. "All clear."

Leo jumped to the ground and a too-quiet Ethan didn't follow. He stayed within touching distance of his mother. Blake knelt beside the open door. "You ready to go into the house, Ethan?"

He peered down from his seat inside the SUV. "Will the bad men come again?"

"This is a good hiding place," Blake said.

Ethan stared at Amanda, and she could barely swallow around the emotion filling her throat, but she made herself smile. "We'll keep you safe, little man."

"Leo's waiting for you," Blake said with a smile that exuded confidence.

Everything in his face, his posture his words screamed certainty. Could he really be sure they were safe here?

Leo barked and Ethan gave a weak smile. "Okay." He climbed out of the vehicle but hovered near the door. "Are you coming, Mommy?"

She pasted on a smile. "Of course." She climbed out and held her hand to him. He grabbed it.

Blake led them into the house. "How about we make chili for dinner?"

"I like spicy," Ethan said, staring at the floor.

Blake raised a brow. "Really? How hot?"

"He downed a box of Red Hots at two years old. He pops jalapeños like they're candy."

"Whew. Hot it is." Blake headed to the kitchen and pulled down a pot.

"Mommy doesn't like spicy," Ethan said, his voice worried.

He gripped Amanda's hand as they followed Blake. Her heart cracked at the loss of laughter she'd witnessed less than an hour before. Why was this happening? Why couldn't the fear just go away?

"Don't worry, Ethan. I'll take care of your mom." Blake pulled some ground meat from the freezer, popped it into the microwave and grabbed some seasonings from the cupboard. "She gets a special bowl." Blake turned toward Ethan. "Do you see any jalapeños?"

He glanced up at Amanda, and she nodded, easing Ethan forward with a gentle push. "I bet they have some."

Ethan examined the cupboard. He took out a can and handed it to Blake.

"Thanks." He tossed the peppers into a small pan. "You want to help me make the chili?"

Ethan nodded and bit his lip.

Blake picked him up and set him on the counter. "You know, buddy, my little boy, Joey, used to make chili with me."

Ethan didn't respond, just poured in a teaspoon of the spice Blake gave him.

"It's pretty scary right now, isn't it?"

The boy nodded and looked over at his mother. Her tremulous smile hurt Blake's heart. He wanted to comfort both of them, but while he'd told Amanda the truth about other investigative possibilities, they were slim. Cops knew better than most how to cover their tracks. He had to believe Vince had sent them here with enough information to save their lives. Every instinct within Blake told him Vince had given Ethan the key to the evidence. He just had to help the boy remember. He hated having to push Ethan, but he had no choice. Not with Vince's house a pile of ashes. They couldn't hide here forever. Eventually someone would track them down.

"Your uncle Vince saved you, didn't he?" Blake said as he showed Ethan how to stir the simmering peppers and spices.

"Blake—" Amanda warned. "I want him to forget."

Blake met her defensive gaze. "Ethan's brave. He can do this."

"Uncle Vince said be brave." Ethan stuck his thumb in his mouth, his legs dangling from the kitchen counter.

Blake grabbed the defrosted meat from the microwave and dumped it into the large pot. "You know what? I forgot to wash my hands. Can you go into the bathroom and wash yours before we get any more germs in our dinner?"

Ethan nodded and Blake set the boy down. As soon as he left earshot, Blake turned on Amanda. "I know you want to protect him, but he saw Vince die. All we can do now is give him the knowledge that justice exists. That the murderers will be punished. He knows who did it, and I think Ethan wants to tell me but he's scared. We have to find out why."

She sucked in a deep breath, and Blake crossed the room and clasped her hands in his. "I won't hurt him, Amanda, but I need him to remember. For his future. And yours."

Her sad eyes broke his heart, but she gave him a slight nod. He let out a slow breath at the small show of faith.

The meat sizzled as Ethan came into the room. He walked straight to Blake. "It's cooking. I can hear it. I want to help."

He lifted the boy on to the counter. "How can I make chili without my number one assistant?"

He smiled, and for several minutes Blake just let the boy stir. "You were very brave the night your uncle was hurt. I need you to be brave again. Can you do that? Can you help us?"

Ethan shook his head violently side to side, his eyes filled with tears. Amanda started across the kitchen, but

Blake held up his hand, stopping her. He faced Ethan. "I'm not going to let anything happen to you or your mom. If that means we go live far away from here, then we'll do it."

Ethan stared at Blake. "You won't let them hurt Mommy?"

"Who said they'd hurt your mommy?"

"The man with the boots." Ethan sucked in a shuddering breath and looked around the room. He pulled Blake's head down close. "He told Uncle Vince if anyone talked, they'd die."

Ethan buried his face into Blake's arms. Ethan's shaking body tore at Blake's soul.

"When you talk, you die," Ethan whispered.

Amanda choked down a sob. Blake fought to control the anger boiling deep inside. He held Ethan just far enough away so he could see every expression playing on the boy's face.

"Do you believe I can protect you?" he asked, praying he'd gained the little boy's trust.

Ethan thought for a moment, biting his lip. "You saved me from the tractor," he said solemnly. "You saved me and mommy from the bad men. You took us away from the police."

Finally, he nodded his head.

"Then, I need you to tell me the truth. No matter how scared you are." Blake placed his hands on the boy's shoulders. "Do you know who hurt your uncle?"

Ethan looked away. "A man with funny boots. Uncle Vince said he was a policeman."

"Did Vince say the man's name?"

Ethan shook his head. "I snuck out after the man left. Uncle Vince was hurt. He told me to go to Blake." Ethan looked up. "That's you."

"That's me. Did he say anything else?"

Ethan wrinkled his nose in thought. "Joey's in the clouds."

Blake rubbed his forehead and a wave of pain washed through him. Why had Vince mentioned Joey? It didn't make sense. Unless he was trying to make sure Blake helped them.

"Why were the man's boots funny?"

"They had dragons. Like in the stories Mommy reads me."

"Custom-made," Blake mused. He smiled at Ethan. "You did good, buddy. I'll get the bad guys, Ethan."

"Keep Mommy safe." The boy frowned in worry and fear.

Blake looked over at Amanda, at her pale face and delicate features, her haunted expression. "Whatever it takes."

Chapter Nine

The lieutenant slumped back in his leather chair and hitched the heel of his custom-made boots over the stone hearth while the fire crackled in front of him. He'd commissioned the dragon design from a craftsman in Dallas. Despite the risk, he'd never go east of the Mississippi for a pair of boots.

"They're not on the Triple C Ranch, but Logan knows something." Johnson's voice filtered through the phone.

No way they could let Logan Carmichael get away with his silence. No matter what government alphabet soup he came from.

"Get our friends at the Department of Public Safety to review Carmichael's P.I. license, taxes, anything you can. Find something. *Adjust* the information. He almost lost his family's ranch once. Let's see how he reacts when he's faced with losing his home again."

"That'll take time."

"No excuses. He needs to learn who to get involved with and who to avoid." The lieutenant stared at the original Remington hanging on the wall of his library. He'd fed the story that his father had invested in Apple before the iPod to explain away the painting and the remodel. Anyone who counted believed him. "What about Blake's mother?"

"We checked out her house. Saw signs that she left in a hurry. Half-eaten breakfast, back door unlocked."

"Stake it out. Take care of her. Blake needs to know we mean business." He swirled a hundred-year-old finger of cognac. Now down to the real business. The real risk to everything he'd built. "Whose bright idea was it to send our man to blow up Vince's house with Blake and the Hawthorne woman inside?"

The phone went silent. The lieutenant smiled. Fear and uncertainty were great motivators.

"You said you wanted the boy alive and the evidence destroyed. Blake and Amanda were expendable."

Johnson was so easily intimidated. His voice trembled. It should.

"The situation has changed. Who ordered it? No, let me guess. Farraday likes large fires and explosions. He doesn't know the meaning of the word *subtle*. You inform him he gets a free pass this time. One more mistake, though, and he pays."

Johnson cleared his throat. "Sir, this is getting out of hand."

"Do I pay you to think?"

"No, sir."

The lieutenant could picture the wimp cringing. One thing about Farraday, he might barrel in, but he had some guts. Johnson's conscience put him on a suspect list that made the lieutenant's gut burn.

"I didn't think so. Our forensic computer expert found some very interesting evidence in *my* system." He rose and hurled the priceless crystal tumbler into the fire. Flames flared as the cognac hit.

"We have a mole. You and Farraday wouldn't have any idea about that, would you?"

"No, sir." Johnson's voice shook.

"Change of plans," the lieutenant barked. "I need to know who betrayed me. I need the evidence. I want them alive—for now. And Johnson, keep Farraday under control. You're partners. What happens to one, happens to the other."

"But—"

"No excuses. I'm taking care of your loose ends. By tomorrow night, we'll have Redmond and the Hawthornes cornered. Amanda Hawthorne's life on the run won't end well. Sometimes, the good guys have to shoot to kill.

"Before they die, though, we get what we want. If they don't give us the evidence…" the lieutenant paused "…we take them apart piece by piece until they do. Starting with the boy. A few screams from her kid should convince even Blake to spill his guts."

AMANDA TOOK ONE LAST LOOK at Ethan snuggled in bed with Leo at his side. He would miss the dog. Maybe, once they settled… She closed the door quietly not wanting to think about the future ahead of them.

"Is he out?"

She started at Blake's voice but nodded. "He's had a long day."

"I contacted Logan. He's looking into the boots."

Amanda didn't want to face Blake. She knew what she had to do, and he wouldn't like it. She didn't respond to him; she simply shrugged into the oversize coat and walked onto the back porch. The chill of the night stung her cheeks.

Blake followed as she expected. She could feel the warmth of his body standing too close behind her. Everything was happening so fast. Her life falling apart, but more than that, the way Blake had wrapped himself around her heart. She'd miss his nearness. Even preparing for a confrontation, she took comfort in his strong presence.

She stared into the night, the stars glittering like twinkling diamonds on an endless black field. "Ethan and I are taking off in the morning," she said, her voice a whisper, although the words shouted into the dark.

"I wondered what had been going on in that head of yours. You were too quiet on the plane." Blake clasped her shoulders and turned her to face him. "Don't run yet. We have another lead."

She couldn't let him convince her to stay. "We *thought* Vince had the evidence. There are too many uncertainties. I'm sorry. My gut tells me to go. I have to think about Ethan."

"You'll look over your shoulder the rest of your life."

"Not if I'm smart and careful."

His glittering eyes bored into her. "You'll be alone. Unable to trust anyone."

"I've been alone for a long time."

"Not anymore," Blake said.

He leaned closer. She could barely breathe, his big body overwhelmed her so. She didn't want to look at him. He squeezed her shoulders and didn't speak. Finally, she raised her gaze.

"You really want to run?" he asked.

"I don't see a choice."

"Then you'd better get ready for company because I'm going with you. You're stuck with me, Amanda. I'm not letting you out of my sight. Not until these men are caught."

He pulled her close to him and she trembled, shaking her head, her forehead rubbing against his wool sweater. "You can't. You have a life here. A town that needs you. Family."

"I lost my son to these men. I won't let the same happen to you. You don't get to decide this, Amanda. If you leave without me, I'll track you down."

She tried to tug away, but he trapped her against the railing, the scent of his aftershave wafting over her and making her head spin with temptation.

He lowered his head to her ear. "You can't stop me," he whispered, his breath warm against her face. "You need me."

"It's not fair to you," she said, trying to resist the emotions overwhelming her the closer he pressed. "Ethan is my responsibility."

"Joey was mine," Blake said. "And I would have done anything not to lose him. Even take help. Will you?"

She clutched his sweater in her fists, her heart aching. "Why are you doing this? I just don't understand. You could wash your hands of us right now. Go back to your life."

"I knocked out a cop for you, honey. Remember? I was there when Vince's house burst into flames. I'm on the run, too. There's a lot more evidence now than the Austin cops had before. And they almost sent me to jail then."

"Tell them I made you break in. Tell them I threatened you."

He laughed. "You believe they'd accept my being coerced by a little thing like you?"

A frigid gust of wind snaked its way beneath her coat. She shivered. "I'm trying to do the right thing, Blake. I'm afraid," she said. "For Ethan. And for you."

His face softened. "I know, but you can't give up, Amanda. Not yet. We're closer than we've ever been."

He pulled her into his arms, holding her against him, warming her from the inside. "Besides," he said, his voice low and husky, "I don't want to say goodbye to you. Not yet."

The growling undertone sent a quiver through Amanda; her nerves exploded to life as his hands rubbed her arms. He enveloped her, and the heat emanating from his body wrapped her in a cocoon.

"You've got me whether you want me or not."

If she ran, he'd keep coming after her. And he'd find her. He was too good at his job.

She sighed. "I'm too tired to fight you anymore. Don't do this."

"What? Warm you?" He bent his head and his lips skirted her cheek. "Touch you?" He hovered over her mouth. "Kiss you?"

She didn't want to resist. For once in her life, why couldn't she have what *she* wanted? Throwing away caution, she grabbed the back of his head and pulled him to her. His lips took hers with certainty. The taste of him made her quake with longing.

"Help me forget," she whispered.

"Then touch me," he whispered. "Show me you want me."

Amanda's hands trembled as she wrapped her arms around him. She pressed herself against his hardening body, her softness crushing against his, soaking up his warmth. Her mouth parted under his and she ventured a taste of his lips, desperate to lose herself in all of her senses.

He swung her into his arms, holding her close and protected, cradled in his embrace. "This time we won't stop." His pulse raced at the base of his neck.

She grasped his sweater. "I don't want you to."

"So be it."

He carried her into the dark and quiet house, flipping the dead bolt before crossing the living room to the bedroom. She let her head rest against his chest. His heart thudded, the rhythm soothing and terrifying all at the same time. When he nudged the door closed, her body thrummed in readiness.

"Last chance," he said, his voice husky.

She touched his lips and stared into his eyes, flaring with want and passion. When had someone ever wanted her as much as Blake?

"Make love to me. Make everything go away for a while," she whispered. For once in her life she wanted someone who wanted her this much.

His eyes burned hot in response to her words. Slowly, he lowered her feet to the floor, but he didn't let her go. He shifted closer. He reached out a hand and laced his fingers through hers before cupping her cheek with his rough palm. He paused, as if waiting for her to pull away. She couldn't. She'd told him the truth. She was past resisting. His gaze held her captive.

His finger-light caress followed her neck and rested against her pulse point. Her heart skipped a beat in response.

"I make your heart race," he said quietly. He clasped her palm and slipped it beneath his sweater, holding it to his chest. "Feel what you do to me, Amanda."

The strong thud, the transparent passion on his face made her quake with want. "Please," she said as she clutched the flannel of his shirt.

The corner of his mouth tilted in satisfaction, but his hand moved slowly, dragging out the anticipation. He lowered his hand to her collarbone, trailed to her shoulder, baring the skin as he pushed aside the soft fleece of the sweatshirt, slipping his hand underneath.

"You're like silk."

Her nipples hardened and, as if reading her mind, his hand moved to the soft mound. He cupped her breast and his thumb flicked against the hard nub. A flash of pleasurable pain clenched in her lower abdomen. Her body sang with each mind-numbing caress.

He pulled away, leaving her panting, throbbing, her body begging for more.

She didn't speak. She grabbed his hand with hers and pressed it back to her breast. "Touch me," she said. "Hold me. Make me feel again."

She'd deal with the consequences of letting herself be vulnerable to him. Tomorrow. Right now she wanted to forget everything, and lose herself in his arms.

"I'm not letting you go."

His voice had gone low, turned into almost a growl. A frisson of anticipation pulsed through her at the intensity of his expression.

He backed her gently to the bed and tugged off her sweatshirt. She sank into the mattress, waiting and wanting. He paused as he looked at her. Bare breasts, nipples hard and begging for him, a bandage surrounding her torso. His gaze lowered and he touched the area of her injury. "Does it still hurt?"

"It's healing."

He lowered his head and tasted the curve of her breast. "Let's see if I can distract you." He closed his mouth over her nipple, and his tongue did things she never imagined possible. She squirmed underneath him as her body pulsed with desire, her legs grew restless. She wanted more.

She gripped his head, pulling him closer, but when

her hand shifted beneath the wool of his sweater and she encountered the flannel material of his shirt, she moaned. "I want to touch you. I want to feel you," she said. "Take it off."

He lifted his head, his hazel eyes blazing with gold. He tugged off the heavy sweater in one motion. She tried to unbutton his shirt, but her hands shook. She couldn't catch hold, and he groaned in frustration.

He struggled with the top button, and for the first time, she realized his hands were shaking, too. He finally worked the button through the hole and drew the flannel over his head. He tossed it to the floor with a grunt and rubbed his hair-roughed chest against her sensitive breasts.

She shivered under him, relishing the feel. Each movement of his body tugged at her insides. Her thighs relaxed and parted. Even with their jeans separating their bare bodies, she could feel the hardness of him pressing against her, begging for entrance.

She caressed his back and tugged him closer, moving against him, trying to ease the ache building higher and higher. The strong muscles rippled beneath her touch. As she clutched at him, his chest vibrated with a low moan.

More than anything Amanda needed his strength, needed those strong arms to hold her close. She wanted, for a brief moment, to feel as if he would never let her go.

Blake lifted his body away, his eyes hooded, his gaze predatory. "If you don't want this, tell me now," he said.

With a trembling hand she touched his lips with her finger. He drew in the digit and bit the tip gently. "You're mine."

He shoved her jeans down her legs, then shucked out of his pants, but not before he snagged a foil packet from his back pocket. "A man has to hope," he said, shooting her an embarrassed smile.

Without giving her time to question or doubt, he rose over her, his entire body shaking with want and need. Blake didn't hide; he accepted his need. When had anyone been willing to show how much he wanted her? With his every touch, he evoked more and more sensation until finally she couldn't feel herself anymore. It was only them.

"Please," she panted as he nestled between her parted thighs. "Now."

"With pleasure." He prepared himself then sank inside her. His body shuddered. "You are beautiful."

She was whole. For the first time. She wrapped her arms and legs around him. He settled into a rhythm that took her spinning outside of herself. Everything he gave she returned until her body tightened. His pace quickened. With a groan of completion he sagged against her just as she fell over into an abyss of pleasure.

They were one, and she would never be the same again.

She didn't know how much time passed before he kissed her shoulder and slowly moved to her side. For a moment, his absence chilled her, then he tucked her against his shoulder. "You're amazing."

Her body shook from more than the passion as his warmth seeped into her. Her heart clung to him, trusted him. She'd given him more than her body. He owned a piece of her soul.

What had she done?

She shivered in his arms as he comforted her, whispered to her. How could she ever leave after that? But how could she not? She cared too much to see him hurt.

His touch lightened as Amanda feigned sleep.

She'd made everything worse. Before this moment, she'd only imagined what Blake could mean to her.

Now she knew.

DAWN'S LIGHT FILTERED through the window slats. Blake had tried to sleep. He failed. He didn't know how long he'd lain there with Amanda's body pressed against his. She'd pretended to fall asleep. He'd let her.

Finally, she hadn't been able to fight any longer. She'd drifted off, but he'd stared endlessly at the ceiling. She'd stunned him.

Every kiss, every caress last night had melted away his frozen heart. She'd tugged at something deep within him he'd thought long dead. He'd wanted to wrap her and hold her tight, but she'd pulled inside herself even as he'd held her in his arms.

Now her body shifted away. He wanted to tug her back against him, to make her forget. For a few moments of bliss, she'd been all his. She'd given him everything.

He'd never had a more generous lover.

Until the fog of passion had rolled away with the light of day.

"You're just going and leave me lying here?"

She sat on the edge of the mattress reaching for her clothes, and her back tensed. "I need to check on Ethan."

She slipped on the sweatshirt, protecting herself from his gaze. The move shouldn't hurt, but it did. He dragged her down and settled her on his hardening body.

"What's that dangerous mind of yours planning, Amanda?"

He pushed aside the wild hair, but she wouldn't meet his gaze. He settled her hips against his and her eyes widened.

"Yeah, I want you again, but not before you tell me what you're thinking."

Her body softened. He could make her purr, but he'd realized he didn't want just a woman who melted in his arms. He wanted a woman who trusted him, who was willing to admit she needed him as much as he needed her.

God, he was falling for her.

And if he said one word, he worried she might bolt out of his arms and out of his life. He couldn't allow that to happen. No matter what. Not until she and her son were safe.

He cupped her face. "Tell me. I can take care of you."

"That's just it. You're not my prince charming, Blake. I don't want you to be. I had enough of that from my ex."

"I'm nothing like Carl." The idea that she'd compare him to that low-life criminal…

"No, you're not. He promised a lot, but when push came to shove, my prince had feet of clay. He hurt Ethan."

Blake's heart tightened. "He hit his son?"

"He ignored him. He hasn't seen Ethan in almost two years."

"What has that got to do with me?"

"He promised me the world. I believed him. I let him take over." She stared down at him. "If I stay and we fight this, if I trust you, you have to trust me, too. No more secret plans with Logan. Vince was my brother. I knew him better than anyone. I can help."

She'd turned the tables on him. The spark in her cobalt eyes made his body leap in response.

"Fair," he said, tugging her to him and tumbling her back on top of him. He pressed her hips against his hardening body.

"How about we seal this deal?"

She straddled his hips, leaning over him.

"Mommy?" Her son's voice and a tentative knock filtered from the hallway.

She sagged over him. "I'll be right there, Ethan," she called through the door.

Blake leaned up and kissed her hard. "We *will* continue this. Later."

She swallowed and her gaze softened. "Later." She slipped into her clothes and gave him one last look. "Partners?"

"Partners." He shrugged into his shirt as Ethan called out again. "You'd better check on him. I'm going out to the barn. I have a few chores to take care of." He slipped on his jeans just as she opened the door. "Amanda—"

She turned back, and he crossed the room. He pushed her curls from her face. "Thank you for believing. I know it wasn't easy, but we're doing the right thing."

Her smile didn't quite reach her eyes. He recognized the doubt, and it stung. Seconds later, it was gone, though, and she smiled. "Right. We'll find the evidence Vince hid. We have to."

She opened the door.

"I'm hungry, Mommy. Why did you sleep so long?"

She led Ethan off to the kitchen, and Blake shoved his feet into his boots. If he was going to live up to his promise, he needed to track down the dragon boots.

He shrugged into his coat and grabbed the phone Logan had given him. He powered it on and walked to the barn. A text message flashed. *Call.*

Blake dialed the number.

"You safe?" Logan asked.

"For the moment."

"Blake, these guys mean business. They've mired

me in threats and paperwork. They're searching every-where, including the cabin. Parris took your mother to an alternate location. Didn't even tell me where."

"But she's safe?"

"As protected as she'll be around Parris." Logan chuckled.

"What the hell are you talking about?"

"Let's just say the heat between those two rivals what's sparking between you and that pretty redhead of yours."

"You're imagining things," Blake said.

"I don't think so. I recognize the symptoms," Logan said. "I also recognize the danger signs."

"I'm handling it," Blake said, even though his lips still tasted of Amanda's sweetness. "Why did you really call?"

"Received a message from Shaun O'Connor. He wants to talk."

"I know him. Thought he was a good cop. But I thought Vince was a good cop, too."

"He says there's some bad stuff coming down. That he has information."

Blake's hair stood up on the back of his neck. Could this be a break? "What do you think? He on the right side?"

"My sources say he's straight. Then again, my sources don't know who the mastermind is."

Blake scratched his chin. He didn't want to get Amanda's hopes up. If the lead panned out, he might be able to end this without causing her more disappoint-ment. He looked back toward the house. "How secure is this phone, Logan?"

"My technogeek expert guaranteed it can't be traced. Except by him."

"Is he that good?"

"I hired him."

"Give me his number. I'll set up a meet."

Chapter Ten

Ethan tugged on Amanda's shirt as she slipped bread in the toaster. "Where's Sheriff Blake going?"

She ruffled her son's head and scanned him up and down. "Don't even think about heading to that barn. It's cold and I see your bare toes."

He wiggled his feet and clutched the dog's fur. "Leo doesn't have shoes."

"He always has a coat. Now scoot. Get dressed, and by the time you get back I'll have breakfast."

"What if I—"

"The sheriff is doing important work."

She rifled through the freezer and found some sliced ham, defrosted it and set the meat on to cook. If they stayed here much longer, they'd have to make a run for supplies.

With a quick flip, their breakfast started to sizzle. Amanda shifted the kitchen curtains aside. Blake had left the barn door slightly open, but she couldn't see him.

If he did chores, wouldn't the teenager the Maddoxes paid notice? She bit her lip. Blake had been so careful keeping them hidden.

As she considered going outside, Ethan scurried into the kitchen, dressed and hungry, Leo at his heels. After she'd fed him, she took another look out the window.

"Can I go outside?" Ethan pleaded.

She sighed. "Sorry, little man. How about we set up a fort in your room?"

"Will you play with me?"

"For a while."

Amanda helped Ethan make the tent, and soon her son and Leo were defending the world against the bad guys.

She knelt beside the draped blanket. "You promise not to go outside unless you tell me?"

Ethan looked up at her and nodded while he tied a sheet around Leo's neck, turning the patient dog into a superhero.

"Okay, then. I'll be in the other room."

He didn't answer, and Amanda closed the door behind her. Blake hadn't come back. With a sigh she veered to the kitchen to grab some coffee, then paused by Maddox's office. A computer sat on the desk.

She stopped and stared at the machine. Had Vince sent her clues in the emails over the last few months that she hadn't recognized? They were few and far between, but maybe, just maybe.

Blake hadn't come back from the barn, but partners didn't sit around and wait. She had to prove to Blake she *could* help. She settled in front of the keyboard, booted up the machine and typed in the web-mail address that Vince had set up for her when she moved in.

She scanned the emails. Tons of junk mail. Typical.

Then Vince's name popped up. Her heart twisted, flashing on her last memory of him. Lying in a pool of blood. She shook away the image.

"Oh, Vince. Help me. Please."

She did a double take. The email was unread. She glanced at the time. Just one day before he'd been killed.

With a shuddering breath she opened the message.

I love you, Sis. Tell Blake I'm sorry.

And a link.

Her heart thudding, she clicked on it. A dialogue box popped up requesting a password.

She entered the only one she had—her email password.

A large warning message flashed on the screen.

You have entered an incorrect password. After three attempts, this file will be destroyed.

Amanda stared at the words. If Vince hadn't used that password, what could he have used? She was no computer expert. And she'd used up one attempt. Blake would be furious. They were supposed to work together.

After a quick check on Ethan, who now had the long-suffering dog in a makeshift jail, she grabbed her coat and trudged into the freezing cold to the barn.

As she slipped through the open door, she caught sight of Blake's backside, and his broad shoulders covered by the shearling coat. She knew what was under his clothes. He looked better without them.

Blake slapped a harness hanging on the wall. "If I bring her and the boy in, what guarantee do I have?"

The words punched Amanda in the gut. No. It wasn't possible. Blake couldn't be arranging to turn them in. She'd believed him. She'd bought every line he'd sold. She'd made love with him. She rushed over and grabbed the phone, quickly ending the call. "What are you doing? What happened to partners? You *lied* to me?"

He winced at the accusation but didn't deny it. "I was trying to find a way to keep you safe."

She sagged back onto a bale of hay. "I can't believe you did this." Amanda couldn't find the energy to be angry. The disappointment froze her insides. "I thought I could trust you. You were supposed to trust me."

Blake's lips thinned, but he didn't respond. What could he say?

She let out a shuddering breath and slipped the phone into her pocket. "Who were you talking to?"

"Shaun O'Connor."

At least he didn't try to prevaricate. She rolled the name around in her head. "I know him. From Austin?"

"He's Internal Affairs. He *says* he's been investigating the precinct for almost a year."

"Before you—"

"Yeah. Needless to say I was very interested."

"What if he's involved? What if he's just trying to find us?"

"Do you really believe I'd put you at risk?" Blake slapped his Stetson against his thigh, punctuating his frustration. "Shaun called Logan. He says he's close to identifying the person responsible. He wants our help."

"I don't know."

Blake sank down beside her on the hay. He folded her hands in his. "Putting you in protective custody gets you out of the crossfire. It keeps you safe while I investigate more. If we have someone on the inside, we have a better chance of catching them."

"What if he's working for the killer?"

The sound of whipping rotor blades roared above them. Blake ran out of the barn. Amanda followed and stared up into the sky, stunned.

Blake shoved her back inside and pulled a rifle off the barn wall. He loaded a cartridge. "Stay behind me."

"How did they find us?" Her stomach clenched. "Ethan! This can't be happening again."

"Listen to me, Amanda. That's a civilian chopper."

She gave him a blank look.

"No bulletproof glass. I can take her down with a .22. If I do it right, we can question the men inside."

Blake gripped the stock of the rifle and stepped into the open.

"Come on. Come back toward me," he muttered.

As if listening to his voice, the chopper circled the ranch house then turned toward the barn. She could see two men through the glass. Blake took aim. Amanda covered her ears.

Just as the chopper veered sharply, the shot echoed through the cold. The pilot slumped over. Frantic, the man beside him tried to grab the controls. Amanda watched in horror as the helicopter tipped and headed for the ground. It plunged with a crash and exploded into flames.

A string of curses erupted from Blake. He raced toward the burning pile of twisted metal, but there was nothing to be done. The men inside couldn't have survived.

He turned back to Amanda. "Go get Ethan. Our location has been compromised. We're leaving."

Before she could go, he reached into her pocket and tossed the cell phone into the flames. "That's it. We can't trust the police at all."

AMANDA PEEKED THROUGH the window of the SUV as Blake strode into the old motel's front office. Ethan sat on the floor in the backseat with Leo, clinging to the dog's fur.

Within minutes he was back. He opened the door and slid behind the steering wheel.

"Room 8."

"Should I even ask if we'll be safe?" Amanda said,

studying the run-down hotel with a skeptical eye. It looked like a strong punch could break down any of the doors.

Blake winced. "They let me pay cash and they don't require a credit card. That's as safe as we can be right now."

Blake pulled the SUV around the back, out of sight of the road. "Let's go," he said.

Amanda grasped Ethan's hand and they entered the room. Shabby furniture, but at least it was clean.

One bed.

"I'll get a cot or rollaway or something," he said. "You and Ethan take the bed." He snagged the ice bucket and left the room.

Amanda shivered in the chilled air and strode to the radiator. She knew the type. She'd fought with it in one of the crummy apartments she and Carl had rented. Within a few minutes, she had the ancient piece of equipment working. Blake returned with a load of bedding.

"No rollaway, but we'll make do."

Amanda grabbed a blanket from the top of the stack and wrapped it around Ethan. She sank into the over-soft mattress and rubbed her arms. "How do you think they found us?"

"Electronics are the only way, so I guess it had to be the cell. Even though Logan said the phone couldn't be tracked, maybe O'Connor has a technogeek who can do it. I can't think of any other way."

Amanda flashed on the time she spent at the keyboard and swallowed. "I used the Maddoxes' computer to get on the internet."

Blake whirled around.

"What?" She glared at him. "I thought I could help."

"When did you turn it on?"

"Right after you went out to the barn. I was on for a while."

"The internet can be like a pointer if you know what you're doing. What were you thinking, Amanda?"

"Don't yell at my mommy." Ethan hopped up and stood, feet apart, challenging Blake.

Blake knelt in front of her son. "Sorry, buddy. You're right."

Ethan sent Blake a censuring look before returning to Leo.

"Why would you do that?" Blake said quietly. "What did you think you could search?"

"Vince's emails. He set up the account when we moved in."

"They must have his accounts tagged." Interest flared in Blake's eyes. "What did you learn?"

She glanced at Ethan who seemed distracted. "Vince sent me an email the day before he was killed," she whispered. "Just a link, but I couldn't open it." She told him about the warning message.

"That has to be the evidence."

"It's no good if we don't have a password."

"With only two tries left, we can't take any chances. I'll go pick up a prepaid cell and call Logan. He has a geek on his staff who might be able to help." Blake stroked the stubble on his chin. "Maybe O'Connor *is* on the up-and-up."

"We can't risk involving the cops. Please don't call him. No more secrets." She grabbed the collar of his coat. "You promised."

"The same goes for you," Blake said with an arched brow. "Deal?"

Looking over her shoulder at Ethan, she nodded.

Blake tipped his Stetson in agreement and walked out the door. Amanda stared after the closed oak, the room suddenly losing its warmth. And not because the heater had failed. How had she come to rely on him so much—his strength, his determination—that when he left she felt his loss all the way through her?

"Was Blake mad, Mommy?"

Ethan came over and leaned into her, as if sensing she needed the comfort.

She lifted him to her lap. "He's trying to catch the bad guys, and I'm trying to help."

"They keep coming after us. Maybe we should hide. Like in hide and go seek," Ethan said logically.

"That's kind of what we're doing here." Amanda focused on her son, but her mind wandered to a terrifying truth. If these guys had been able to track them in the middle of nowhere, how could she have ever expected to disappear? Really disappear. If she hadn't come to Blake, she didn't want to think about what would have happened to her, but more importantly, to Ethan.

"Blake will make it better, Mommy. He's big. He saved me from the tractor."

Ethan patted her cheek in comfort, then scurried across the room and tried to run over Leo's wagging tail with his truck.

She wished she'd had time to review more of Vince's emails. Maybe there was a clue to the password in there, and if they found the evidence, maybe Ethan would have a chance at a real life. She stared at her son. The longer this went on, the more fragile their lives felt. Amanda didn't know how long she wrestled with the unpleasant options before Blake returned, carrying three phones.

"I'm not taking any more chances. We're dumping these after each use," he said.

She looked at the man who had driven her to passion the day before. He was a warrior now, a fighter. He would keep them as safe as he could.

She bit her lip. "I've been thinking. About the future. When we catch these guys, will Ethan still have to testify?"

Blake's entire body stilled. He turned to her. "If Vince really did have that evidence, and if we can find a way to access it, maybe not. I can't promise, though."

"I want Ethan to have a normal life."

"He will."

"I've got a bad feeling, Blake. We're at a motel, out in the open. We don't have a computer to follow Vince's emails." She clutched at his arm. "If anything bad happens, you have to save Ethan first. Promise me."

His jaw clenched and his eyes grew cold. "It won't come to that."

She pressed her hand to his cheek and held his gaze with hers. "Promise me."

He glanced over at the boy wrestling with Leo. "Ethan first." The words dragged out reluctantly, but in his clear hazel eyes she saw his vow.

She let out a sigh of relief. "What do we do?"

"We call Logan." Blake pulled out one of the new cell phones and tugged her toward the bathroom.

Amanda shot a sharp glance at Ethan, but he was busy tickling Leo. "Little man, Blake and I will be in here."

Her son barely looked over. "Okay, Mommy."

Blake closed the door behind them, pressed the speakerphone button and dialed Logan's number.

"Carmichael."

Logan sounded stressed. He'd barked his name through the phone. She sent Blake a concerned glance.

He frowned as if he too hadn't expected quite that re-action from his friend.

"It's Blake."

A curse sounded through the phone, and a chill ran down her back.

"What's going on?" Blake asked, tugging her toward him as if he had to keep her close.

"You really pissed off somebody with some pull in Austin. They're coming after me with both barrels. They falsified records. They're trying to shut down the ranch and confiscate everything, including my funds."

Amanda rubbed her temple. She'd brought this di-saster on everyone. She raised her gaze to Blake. He leaned back against the sink and closed his eyes. "Hell, I'm sorry, Logan."

Logan let out a grunt. "Not as sorry as they're going to be once I get through with them," he said. "They have no idea what I can do. Once we find out who's behind this, my response will be…appropriate."

Blake's mouth quirked a bit. She stared at him, stunned. Who was Logan Carmichael? He wasn't some-one she'd want to be on the wrong side of, that's for sure.

"We're on the same page there," Blake said, toying with the neckline of her sweatshirt, baring her collar-bone, running his fingers along the fragile bone. She shivered as the awareness between them built.

"Amanda discovered a link that Vince sent via email. It's password-protected. We don't know how to access it. You got a guy?"

"The best. Give me the email info."

Amanda bent over and provided the account infor-mation. "Is that enough?"

"Should be plenty," Logan said.

"Could be how they tracked us to Maddox's," Blake

warned. "A helicopter's burning up on the west side. The pilot veered just as I tried to bring them down with a shot. It's a mess."

"Fire department's already out there." Logan paused. "Have you heard from your mother?"

Blake stilled his caresses, his forehead creased in concern. "No. I had to ditch your phone. Are you telling me you don't have her location?"

"I haven't found them. Yet. I will. But I've got to keep the Austin PD busy. I don't want to provide anyone else too much information if possible. Too many opportunities for leaks with all these unknown players."

Blake rubbed the back of his neck. "I'm cornered, Logan. I need intel."

"I'll do what I can. By the way, we tracked the boots to a small shop in Dallas. Paid with cash. The guy used an alias. We're working on it."

"Get pictures of all the cops in the Austin PD. See if the owner recognizes any of them. I'll check back in an hour. And Logan, make sure Mom's okay. These guys are escalating. Taking too many chances."

"You got it."

Blake ended the call and met her gaze. She could see the worry in his eyes.

"Parris is a good cop. You told me so yourself."

"He's a great deputy, but these guys have firepower he's never faced."

She rested a hand against his chest and leaned into him. "He's probably doing exactly what you are. Hiding in the most unlikely place." She glanced at the cracked tub and the faded linoleum floor. "Someday maybe we'll laugh about this."

She bowed her head and he pulled her to him. She sank into his warmth and just rested there, letting him hold her and stroke her back. "I'm so sorry I brought you this trouble. You and Logan. But I thank God you're here."

"This isn't your fault." He hugged her closer. "The criminals in the Austin PD did that. When they decided the law didn't mean anything."

"Until I came to Carder with that ice storm, your life was fine."

His caress stopped. He set her back, and the gold in his eyes sparked with intensity. "My life was on auto-pilot," he said harshly. "I didn't know the truth about Joey and Kathy. I was dead inside. Going through the motions but not living."

He stroked her cheek and twirled her curls around his finger. "You helped me feel again. You brought me back to life, Amanda."

"And ruined it in the process. Your house is shot up. Your mother is missing. Your best friend is in trouble."

"Once we catch Vince's killer, everything will work out."

She caressed the stubble on his cheek. "How can you believe that with everything going on?" She sagged against him. "I want to just run away and leave this all behind." The overwhelming weight of what they faced crushed her. "I can barely breathe. I can't see a way out."

Blake hugged her tightly to him. "Shh. I know you're scared, but you're not alone. You have me, and I won't let you go until you're safe."

"Why?"

He clasped her hand and turned her palm to his lips. "Because I have something I want when this is over." Blake's eyes sparked with awareness. He pulled her hips to him, setting her against his hard body. The bathroom closed in, the sparks between them caught fire.

Her breath caught. He stroked at the pulse point of her neck with his callused finger. Her heart jumped and he smiled.

"So responsive," he whispered.

"Ethan," she said softly.

"He's busy with Leo. Besides, I only want a taste."

Amanda sighed as he lowered his mouth, ever so slowly. Too slowly. She wanted to tug him to her, but he'd pinned her arms to her side.

Then, just as his lips touched hers, he let out a primal groan and crushed her mouth under his. He didn't hesitate, but plundered and explored. He pressed her closer and his leg parted her thighs, creating a friction that made her shudder.

"That's more than a taste," she panted, her voice husky.

The wicked gleam in his eyes told her he didn't care. He pressed her back against the wall. "Maybe more like an appetizer."

He lowered his mouth to her neck, then pushed aside the sweatshirt and bared her shoulder. With one hand he cupped her breast and she moaned, her body trembling beneath his caress.

Her response amazed Blake. He flicked her nipple and it hardened beneath his hand. She was a woman he could lose himself in. It didn't matter what was going on around them.

He wanted to forget for a moment the large battle facing them. If they couldn't get Vince's password, it would take much longer to uncover the identity of the traitor cops. He'd have to send Amanda and Ethan away.

She clutched his arms and nipped at his neck. His heart thudded against her. He didn't want to give her up.

But he would…if it meant saving her. He wouldn't lose someone he cared for. Not again.

Her hands splayed across his back and dipped beneath his shirt. Her bare fingers on his skin sent his desire into overdrive. What would happen if he just picked her up and took her? Right here, right now?

The way his body leaped at her touch, he wouldn't maintain control for long.

Her fingers lingered at the button of his jeans.

"Do you want the main course," he whispered in her ear. "Because I'm ready."

Blake's ringing phone shocked him out of his passionate haze. With shaking hands he fumbled for the phone. "How did you get this number? I blocked it."

Amanda tugged at his wrist and pressed the speakerphone button. Blake sighed and held the phone between them.

Logan laughed. "Who do you think you're talking to?"

"If you can do it—" Blake began.

"Hi there, Amanda," Logan interrupted smoothly. "I have the best techy in the business, but don't call anyone else with this phone. Because they probably tracked you through the computer's internet service provider, they aren't tech dumb." He paused. "Which brings me to a problem."

"You opened the file."

"No. Let me put Zane on."

"Sheriff Redmond?" The man's voice was gruff. He sounded like a military trooper, not a geek.

"The file?"

"I have a problem. This guy, Vince Hawthorne? Was he into computers?"

Blake glanced at Amanda and she frowned, the worry

on her face straining her mouth. His gut churned. "Yeah. Said if he hadn't been a cop, he'd have worked for Bill Gates. He liked messing around with stuff."

"I was afraid of that." Zane paused and keys pounded in the background. "He was good. Better than good. I won't go into the technogarbage, but I can't break the code on the file. I've got no access. It's in the clouds, but if we don't have the right password…"

"What, it'll self-destruct in five seconds?"

"Well, the equivalent."

Blake couldn't believe this. Couldn't they catch a break? Amanda groaned and dropped her head against his chest. He stroked her hair.

"There's got to be a way. It's just a bunch of ones and zeroes."

"Well, they don't mean squat if the numbers aren't in the right order. From what I can see, Vince did a number on this file. Unless we enter the correct password, the data will be so corrupted, I don't think a supercomputer could decode it. He should've been working for the CIA. I'm sorry."

Blake wanted to punch the wall. Damn Vince. Amanda's face had paled. He couldn't let her see his own frustration, although somehow he got the impression over the last few days she'd learned to read him more than most.

"Okay, we have no choice. We have to find the password. Any suggestions?"

"Could be anything. Letters, numbers, symbols. Did Vince give you any hints?" Zane asked.

"He was killed before he could tell anyone anything, except maybe Ethan. And I don't have a computer. Zane, maybe you can find something in those emails Vince sent to Amanda."

"I'll have him check it out."

Blake pressed Amanda closer to him. He had to start thinking contingency. "Logan, we're going to need fake I.D.s. If something doesn't break soon, they won't have a choice but to disappear."

Chapter Eleven

The devastation on Amanda's face echoed in Blake's heart. To keep her safe, he might have to give her up. Or give up making the bastards who killed Joey pay.

The choice didn't bear thinking about.

A knock sounded at the door. "Mommy, I'm hungry."

Amanda rubbed her eyes and straightened her back.

"Be right out, little man," she called out. "We'll get something to eat soon."

Amanda met Blake's gaze, her own somber. "We're running out of options," she said.

"We'll crack the password, and Logan will come through on the boots. It's not over."

"I don't want them to get away with what they've done." Amanda righted her shirt and touched her lips. The lips he'd bruised with his passion.

"Mommy, I'm hungry now."

She sighed. "Ethan, why don't you turn on the television? I'll be right there." She lowered her voice. "I can't distract him much longer. He needs to run and play."

"Hopefully this will be over soon," Blake said. "He's a good boy. You're a good mom."

With a tired sigh, Amanda shrugged, opened the door and walked back into the bedroom. A cat-and-mouse chase blared from the television. Ethan smiled at the antics, although he didn't laugh as much as Blake would have hoped. It would take time.

"You could catch them both, couldn't you, Leo?" Ethan whispered to the dog and buried his face in the animal's fur. "You're a hero."

Blake bent to her ear. "I think Leo's found a new master," he whispered and clasped his arms around her waist, pulling her hips back against him so he could feel her closeness.

"Mommy, Mommy! You're on TV."

Ethan bounced up and ran over to the television set. They hurried over. Amanda's picture flashed on the screen.

"Let's join our on-site reporter for today's latest news story. An arrest warrant has been issued for Amanda Hawthorne. Ms. Hawthorne has been implicated in the murder of her brother, Austin police detective Vince Hawthorne, as well as a car theft and assault on a police officer. She is traveling with her son, Ethan Hawthorne, and Sheriff Blake Redmond of Carder, Texas." Blake cursed as his picture appeared beside Amanda's. "Sheriff Redmond, who was fired from the Austin Police Department under suspicious circumstances, has been identified as a person of interest. Both are considered armed and extremely dangerous. Please do not approach them if you see them. Contact local authorities."

Amanda met Blake's gaze. "This is not good."

"It's worse than that." Blake rubbed the bridge of his nose. "They've just given the entire state the right to shoot us on sight. They either know we don't have the evidence or they decided we aren't worth keeping alive."

"What about Ethan. Surely…"

Blake glanced at her son, the boy's innocent smile as

he played with Leo raking across his heart. "Collateral damage. They won't have to worry about his testifying."

She ran to her son and pulled him into her arms. "What are we going to do?"

"We stay put until we hear from Logan, and we work on the password."

"You're squishing me, Mommy." Ethan squirmed out of his mother's arms and tugged on Blake's shirt. "I'm still hungry."

After shrugging into his shearling coat, Blake pulled his Stetson down over his eyes and tucked the Glock into the back of his jeans. "I'm going to find something to eat." He knelt beside Ethan. "Then, buddy, you and I are going to have a talk. Okay? You ready to be my deputy? Help me catch the bad guys?"

Ethan nodded, his face curious but cautious.

"It'll be okay, Ethan. Trust me."

"But the news," Amanda muttered as she followed him to the door. "You can't risk going out there."

"The story just aired. I'll be low-key, but we need some supplies. Before long, neither of us will be able to go out again." He placed his granddad's .45 at the top of the closet. "Just in case. I'll be back soon. Don't leave the hotel room."

She nodded and he looked back at her. If they didn't catch a break in the case soon, Blake didn't want to think about what their next step would have to be.

ETHAN SAT CROSS-LEGGED in front of the television, scratching Leo's ears. Amanda had tried to talk to him about the night Vince died, but he just shook his head and clamped his lips together. He didn't feel safe without Blake here. Neither did she.

Amanda paced around the room, unable to settle anywhere and paused in front of the television.

"Mommy, you're in my way."

"Sorry, honey." She scooted to the side and glanced at her watch. Blake should be back soon.

A rhythmic knock sounded at the door.

She peered through the peephole and caught sight of Blake's Stetson before unlocking the chain. "I thought you took the key."

The door shoved in, slamming her against the wall. Her head snapped back, and her skull exploded with pain.

Two men in ski masks barreled into the room.

"Ethan! Run!"

Amanda struggled free from behind the door just as the smaller man grabbed Ethan. He screamed and Leo leaped at the man's arm, growling as he clamped down. With a curse, the larger man kicked the dog, forcing him to let go. The man shoved his boot against Leo's side, and he hit the corner of the dresser with a yelp, slumping to the ground, still.

She had to get to the gun. Amanda raced toward the closet. The large man grabbed her by the waist just as she slid open the door.

"Oh no, you don't."

He twisted her around and threw her on the bed. Amanda let her momentum carry her onto the bed, then she rolled to the other side.

"Don't hurt my mommy!" Ethan screamed. He kicked and squirmed in the man's arms, clawing at the four-leaf clover patch on the man's elbow. She jumped on the intruder's back, gripping his hands to pry Ethan loose from his hold.

The kidnapper cursed as meaty hands clutched her

arms and yanked her off the smaller man's back. Desperate, Amanda whirled around and tore off the big man's ski mask. She dragged her fingernails down his cheek drawing blood. He cried out and, with a quick move, pinned her against the wall. He slapped her, and her jaw exploded in pain.

"Put the kid in the trunk," he ordered the other man, his voice soft and oh so cold. "I have some *unfinished* business to take care of."

He smiled at her, his eyes malevolent with purpose.

"Ethan!" she screamed as he was carried out the door, hollering and crying for her. "Don't take my son!"

The smaller man looked back, hesitated, but then Ethan yelled even louder. Frantically, the kidnapper looked right, then left and disappeared out the hotel room door, shoving it closed.

Ethan was gone.

She was alone with the dead-eyed man.

Oh, God. She had to get out of here. She had to get to Ethan.

"Damn it. You took my knee out. You shot me." He put a hand to his bleeding cheek. "You shouldn't have done that," he said softly. "You're going to pay."

The bear of a man momentarily eased his grip, and Amanda raced for the door. He just laughed and grabbed her by the hair, tugging until the pain made her eyes water. He shoved her on the bed and sat on her legs.

Amanda twisted and turned to buck him off. She tried to reach him to scratch his face, but she couldn't. He just smiled and unbuckled his belt.

Frantically, Amanda looked toward the closet. The gun. Could she somehow get to it?

"I saw the .45 up there. You won't get the chance."

The big man slipped the leather strap from the loops. "Good thing hotel clerks watch a lot of TV."

Beefy hands grabbed her by her throat and squeezed. She couldn't breathe. Spots danced in front of her eyes. "We want Vince's evidence. Wait here for a call on the hotel phone. Deliver what we want, or you won't see your kid again."

He held her down with one hand and took out a knife, twisting it in her face, taunting her with the shiny blade.

This couldn't be happening. She couldn't die. She opened her mouth to scream, but no sound escaped the hold he had on her throat. She kicked out her legs, trying to break his hold.

He just laughed.

He lowered the blade.

She closed her eyes.

With a single slice, he cut her sweatshirt down the middle. "You won't ever forget what I did."

Oh, God. Please. No.

BLAKE HAD DITCHED his Stetson and lowered a baseball cap over his brow. He jostled the paper grocery sack in front of his face. He'd been thankful the superstore had been in walking distance. He hadn't wanted to chance exposing the SUV, and a small grocery would have attracted too much attention.

He rounded the corner to the motel. The door to room eight was open.

His stomach fell. He dropped the bag and ran.

Amanda lay in the center of the bed cuffed to the metal headboard with zip ties. Blake's stomach lurched. Her sweatshirt was torn away from her body; dried blood surrounded a cut above her breast. One eye was swollen shut. She didn't move. Leo lay in the corner, still.

Blake raced across the room and with a shaking hand touched her cheek, terrified she would be cool to the touch. She shrank back from him with a whimper. He stilled. Even as his heart cracked in pain, his knees shook in relief. She was alive.

"It's me, Amanda. Blake. I'm going to get these off you." He pulled a pocketknife from his jeans and cut through the plastic.

She whimpered when he eased her arms down to her side. A shuddering breath escaped her bleeding lips, and she pried her eyes open to look at him.

The pain in her gaze hurt his heart. He cupped her face. "Amanda? Can you hear me?"

"Ethan," she croaked, a tear squeezing from the corner of her eye and trailing down her cheek. "They took Ethan. Please find him."

Blake ran out the motel room door, but there was no sign of a car, a van or anything out of the ordinary. Not that he'd expected it. He would've noticed walking up. He grabbed the groceries then closed and locked them in.

"How many?" he asked, sitting next to her on the bed, afraid to get too close, afraid he'd hurt or frighten her.

"Two. Ski masks. I tore one off. Scratched him. Then he did this."

She raised a trembling hand to the mark on her breast. He took her hand in his and covered her chest with the torn shirt. As gently as he could, he threaded his fingers through hers as she told him everything her attacker had said. Chills skittered down his spine with each word. Terror burned behind his eyes. They could have killed her.

"God, I'm sorry. I should never have left you." Sick to his stomach, he walked into the bathroom and leaned over the sink. He gripped the porcelain and wanted to snap it in two. He wished it was the bastard's neck. With a long exhale, he stared at his face in the mirror. He was no closer to discovering who was behind it, and now they'd taken Ethan. The only chance Amanda's son had was a ransom demand…or Logan. Blake took several thin washcloths, walked back into the bedroom and dumped a handful of ice in one of them.

He sat on the bed beside her and settled the ice pack on her swollen eye, then gently washed the blood from her skin. "Did he rape you?" He could barely form the words.

She choked back a sob. "I thought he was going to. Then he marked me with his knife." Amanda covered the curve of her breast where a B-shaped cut marred the pale perfection that he'd kissed and caressed last night. "He wanted me to know who was to blame."

Blake held the anger inside, simmering like dry kindle waiting to flare. The man was dead.

She struggled to sit up. "I'm not important. They want the evidence or they'll…kill…Ethan." She could barely form the words. Her nails bit into his arm, her expression panicked. "We don't have it. What are we going to do? How can we get him back?"

He couldn't comfort her, but as gently as he could, he pressed her back against the bed. Blake scanned her pale face, her bruised face, the cut peeking beneath her torn shirt. "Please, Amanda, take a deep breath. You could have a concussion. I promise I'll find Ethan, but I've got to get you to a doctor."

She met his gaze and shook her head. "We can't afford to get help. I'll live with the headache."

"Okay, okay. At least let me look," he said gently.

She lifted her gaze to him and nodded, the trust in her eyes more than he could stand. He hadn't been there for her. As gently as he could, he checked her scalp, grimacing at the bump, and all the while cursing himself inside. Guilt sliced at his heart. "We can doctor the cut with antibiotic ointment, but you've got a major knot." He pressed lightly at the side of her head. She flinched but didn't cry out as he finished examining her injuries.

Every bruise made him want to shove his fist through the wall.

As he finished, a whine sounded from across the room. Blake lasered on the noise. Leo lay against the wall, licking at what was clearly a broken leg. "Ah, boy." He stood and walked over to the dog. "You tried to save him." Blake rubbed Leo's ears, gave the dog a comforting pat and stood. "You need a vet, and I need backup."

He took out the second cell phone, then paused. Every time he'd called Logan it had ended in disaster. Parris and his mom were missing. Deputy Smithson was in a coma. Ethan had been taken.

He had to wonder. Could Logan have a mole?

He tapped the phone against this jeans, then dialed a number.

"Come on, Mom," he muttered. "Pick up."

Amanda shifted to a sitting position. "No, don't involve her. It's too dangerous."

"Parris is with her. If they can get a message to Logan, they can tell him he's got a leak in his organization. He can take additional precautions."

"What if the problem *is* Logan?" Amanda said quietly. "He could lose his entire business and his ranch if he doesn't play with the police. Maybe he decided—"

"No way. You don't know what Logan's been through. He'd never put a woman and child at risk."

"You trust him that much?"

Blake turned to her, hunched in a position to protect her injured body. He didn't blame her for being skeptical, but he knew his friend's past. He knew the kind of man Logan was. "Without a doubt." He dialed his mother's number again. Straight to voice mail.

He drummed his fingers against the phone. He had no choice, but he could make the call count. He dialed Logan.

"Carmichael."

"Call this number from somewhere secure." Blake let his hand hover over the off button, listening for any telltale clicks to indicate they were being monitored.

"I *am* secure," Logan said.

"I can't be too careful."

"Gotcha."

The phone went silent.

Blake pocketed the phone. "I'm going to refill the ice. You're going to need it."

"You want to talk to Logan without me," Amanda said. "Some partner."

At the ringing phone, Amanda narrowed her gaze at him. Blake pressed the speakerphone button with a sigh. "Ethan's been kidnapped. They hurt Amanda."

Logan let out a string of curses. "Get out of there."

"We can't. They're calling back on the hotel phone with instructions. They want the evidence."

Logan paused. "Take me off speaker."

Blake met Amanda's gaze, then pressed the mute button. "Please," he said. "He needs to feel free to say anything."

She raised her gaze, the pain in her eyes enough to break his heart.

"He thinks Ethan is dead."

Blake could barely hear her words as she choked them out.

"I don't," he said. "They could have killed you both. They still want something." He raised the phone to his ear. "Speakerphone is off," he said into the mouthpiece as he clasped her hand in his, rubbing her palm, trying to give her comfort.

"They *need* the evidence for some reason."

"I know."

"The boy might already be dead."

"I don't think so," Blake muttered. "If I'm them, I want to know what he knows and who he told. Just in case. And I still think Ethan may have the key to the password."

Amanda let out a sob. Blake tucked her against his side, praying she wouldn't feel alone.

"I'm in the dark here, Logan. I need equipment, weapons. We can't just sit and wait until they decide to call."

Amanda clutched his arm. "I need to read those emails again. There's got to be a clue."

"And a computer and internet access."

"You got it," Logan said. "Anything else?"

"I tried calling Mom. She didn't answer."

"We haven't located her. Or Parris. But knowing that cagey old man, they're probably holed up someplace secure."

"Keep looking," Blake said. "I'm getting worried. I need to know they're safe. Any more from Zane?"

"No. I've never seen him so pissed off. Vince must have been really good."

Robin Perini 185

"I never realized. I just thought he liked gadgets. Is there a way to get more than two more tries at that password?"

"Not according to Zane. If he fiddles with it, the thing will turn into unrecognizable bits and bytes."

"If Vince gave the password to Ethan…" Blake met Amanda's gaze and she shut her eyes in pain. He stroked her back. "We won't have the evidence until we find him."

"Let me send backup along with the supplies, Blake."

He rubbed the bridge of his nose where an ache began to throb. "Who do you trust more than anyone?"

"Rafe. He had my back in that mess three years ago. He doesn't quit. He never leaves anyone behind. I should know."

Blake recognized the loyalty. "Okay, send him to the Shady Rest Motel. Room 8."

"That place is a dump."

"There are only a few places that don't take credit cards. This is one of them."

Logan paused and called out to someone. "He can be there in an hour. He wears a patch. Injured his eye in Afghanistan. You can't miss him."

"Thanks, Logan."

"Just find the kid."

"I will."

They ended the call, and Blake felt Amanda's chilled body shiver against him. He walked to the closet. "Bastard took my grandad's Colt," he said, as he grabbed an extra blanket.

"I'm sorry."

"Granddad wouldn't have liked anyone but a Redmond touching it."

Amanda picked up the phone. "It has a dial tone. How long will it take them to call?"

"They'll want us to sweat. They want us to worry."

"I already am."

"Me, too." He sat down beside her. "Let me check the bullet wound."

She nodded, and he lifted her shirt probing at the gash in her side. "It's improved. Not so inflamed. Looks like we treated it enough to fight off the infection." Keeping his touch as gentle as possible, he cleaned the area. "Seems like I spend all my time trying to get you out of your clothes. Don't get me wrong, I don't mind the job," he tried to joke, but the world didn't seem funny right now. He sighed. "I hate seeing you hurt."

He stripped off his sweater, then the flannel shirt beneath it.

"Blake," Amanda began. "I don't think I—"

"As much as I want to make love to you every second of every day, I know that's not what you need," he said quietly. He threw aside the torn sweatshirt and eased her arms into the sleeves of his shirt, rolling them up until her hands peeked through. "This will keep you warm."

He helped her button up, and finally tucked the blanket around her. He slipped into his sweater, then settled on the bed next to her and pulled her against him. He kept his Glock within reach. "Try to rest," he said quietly.

He stroked her auburn hair, the blue in his flannel reflecting in her eyes. "You really are amazing. And beautiful."

She shook her head and pushed back her hair probing her swollen eye with her fingertips. "You're a liar."

"Amanda," he said quietly. "I don't lie."

She ducked her head into his chest. "Do you think Ethan's okay?"

He refused to take her bait. He honestly didn't know. "Ethan's smart. He has more courage than any kid I know."

She gripped his sweater. "There's only one way for this to end, isn't there?"

"The lawman in me wants to arrest the bastards and have them pay for what they've done. The father and lover wants to send them to hell in short order."

She shivered. "I keep seeing that man taking Ethan. They put him in a trunk, Blake. Ethan hates the dark."

She hid her face against his sweater and finally let her tears fall. Each sob wrenched a piece of Blake's soul. He couldn't do anything but wait. Wait on Logan. Wait on the kidnappers. Wait on Rafe.

His prepaid phone rang.

Blake picked it up.

"It's Logan. You got TV, Blake?"

He grabbed the remote. "Yes."

"Turn it on. Oh man, I'm so, so sorry."

Blake's gut turned over. The picture flickered. A photo of his mother's neighborhood stared back at him from the small screen.

"Minutes ago, a charred body was discovered in the smoldering remains of a home in the small community of Carder, Texas. Sources from the fire department say the home belonged to the mother of the local sheriff, Blake Redmond, who is one of the subjects of an ongoing manhunt by the Austin Police Department."

"The body is burned beyond recognition." Logan let out a sigh. "God, I'm sorry."

Chapter Twelve

Amanda's stomach heaved as Blake turned off the television. Her heart shattered into a million pieces. She couldn't think. Couldn't feel. It had to be a mistake. She gripped Blake's sweater. This couldn't be happening.

"Blake, you there?" Logan's voice sounded through the phone.

"Are you sure it's her?" Blake asked, his voice too steady. "Can you find out?"

"I'll try."

"What about Parris? He was with her." Blake shoved a hand through his hair. "I want to know who's responsible."

The ice in Blake's voice made Amanda shudder. His face had gone hard as stone. His eyes turned cold, his arms dropped from around her, he sat on the side of the bed, his back to her. He'd closed off, and she didn't blame him. The world had collapsed around him.

"Blake—" Logan began.

"Don't start. You know what I have to do."

The man on the other end of the phone whispered an order she couldn't make out. "I understand. Rafe's on his way."

"I need to know what happened, Logan."

Blake ended the call and stared at the phone, unseeing. To some he might appear to be perfectly in control, but Amanda knew better. His jaw throbbed and his hand shook. He cared more than any man she'd ever known. He'd put his life and family on the line for her and Ethan. Her eyes burned with tears. Nancy couldn't be dead.

She touched his shoulder, her stroke tentative. "Maybe it's not—"

"Don't." He shrugged her away and stood up.

Amanda had seen Blake angry and frustrated, but she'd never seen the fury vibrating from within in quite this way. He paced the floor like a caged animal, stopping beside Leo, who lay huddled against the wall.

Blake looked up at the ceiling, his fists white with tension. He took one shuddering breath, then another. She wouldn't have been surprised if he shoved his fist through the wall, but he just stood there, shaking, lines of pain etched in his face.

"I need to get out of here," he said, his voice soft. "You don't want to be around me right now."

"Don't push me away." Amanda struggled to stand, swaying slightly. She eased to him. He needed her. She didn't know what she could do, but she could be there for him.

"Amanda—" he warned.

She pressed against his body and wrapped her arms around him. "Let me be here for you."

"I shouldn't have left her." Blake's tortured expression broke her heart. "When you told me about Kathy and Joey, I should have gotten her out of town."

"You didn't know where this would lead. Neither of us did."

"From the day I turned eighteen, I promised my dad that if anything happened to him I'd always take care of her. And I left her. I knew they would do anything.

I should've sent you both away. I should have protected you all. I let this happen."

Amanda lifted her face to his, her chin resting on his sweater. "I'm sorry."

He paused and stared down at her, his gaze clearing for a moment. "This isn't your fault."

The agony on his face broke her heart, but she could say nothing.

"I can't believe she's gone."

He buried his face in her hair, his body shuddering. He squeezed her and she hugged him, stroking his back, whispering to him, holding him tight.

Eventually, after what seemed like hours, he raised his head, his eyes blazing. "I'll make them pay for this. Once we get Ethan back, they'll wish they'd never hurt you or my family."

THE DRAGONS ETCHED on the lieutenant's boots gave Johnson the creeps. They always had.

"You *killed* her?" the lieutenant said. "In *another* burning building?"

The cold look in their boss's eyes froze Johnson in place, a chill of foreboding settling over his heart.

"Blake needed to be taught a lesson." Farraday, his partner, crossed his arms in challenge and faced down the man who'd recruited them. He didn't seem fazed. Didn't seem to mind the lieutenant's anger at all.

Fool.

"You screwed up!" The lieutenant strode to Farraday and grabbed his collar, looked at him in disgust and shoved him away. "I had a plan. A sophisticated plan. We hunt down the murderer of one of our own—his sister—and the sheriff who helped her escape. An ex-Austin cop who we couldn't prove was corrupt, but now we have the evidence. They were killed in the crossfire, and we're devastated because her innocent five-year-old son was killed, too." The lieutenant smiled. "It was perfect. Until you had to go off on your own and *try* to get creative."

He paced back and forth. "Now it looks suspicious. The brass at Internal Affairs is curious. That bastard, Shaun O'Connor is getting close, and I can't block the investigation any longer without raising suspicion. Because *you* were too obvious, Farraday. A helicopter? Real subtle. You're leading them to us."

Farraday shrugged. "I'll figure a way out of it."

The lieutenant picked up the Colt .45 Farraday had stolen from the hotel room. He weighed the weapon in his hands.

Oh, man. Johnson wanted to run, but his feet couldn't move. He'd seen that expression before. Once before. When he'd found out Vince was working with O'Connor.

The lieutenant spun the gun's barrel. "Johnson here said you hurt the Hawthorne woman."

"She deserved it." Farraday shrugged.

The lieutenant cocked a brow.

Farraday shrugged. "Okay, I knocked her around a little. Made my mark. I should have done more. I would have if Johnson hadn't been so squeamish."

"At least Johnson is smart enough to be scared right now. I need Blake and Amanda to bring me that evidence. You just pissed off Blake Redmond. You're a liability, Farraday."

The lieutenant pulled back the hammer on the Colt. He lifted Blake's weapon and before the cop could speak, took the head shot.

The explosion sent brains spewing across the room.

"I don't like stupid people," the lieutenant said. "Leave the mess. We'll pin it on Blake."

A whimper sounded from the corner. "And shut him up. I have a call to make." He slammed out of the room.

Johnson looked at his partner's body. Leave it? Did the lieutenant really think he could pin everything on Blake? Johnson grabbed a soda and a candy bar and strode over to the boy, offering it to the scared kid. Ethan shook his head, buried his face in his arms and rocked back and forth. "Go to Blake. Go to Blake," he whispered.

Johnson didn't like killing old women and kids. Getting a few bad guys put away on less-than-kosher evidence and a few extra bucks for his kids' college funds wasn't worth this.

His boss poked his head back into the room. "Johnson."

He slowly turned and raised his gaze to deadly, cold eyes.

"If you screw up again, I won't be so lenient."

THE HOTEL ROOM HAD closed in on Blake. He wanted to tear West Texas apart and find these guys. He wanted to see his mother's house for himself. He wanted to get Amanda out of this hotel room and far away from here.

He couldn't do any of it. He was stuck, waiting for the men who'd killed his son and his mother to play cat and mouse.

Regret suffocated him, smothering his heart. Maybe if he'd brought her with them... No, he couldn't let himself give in to the guilt. Not yet. He had to stay focused. He had to think of Ethan. His mom would have wanted him to save Amanda's son.

She hovered in the door of the bathroom, her eyes

red and haunted, the bruises turning darker with each passing hour.

To distract himself, he filled another thin washrag with ice. He handed it to her.

She accepted the ice pack from him and pressed it against the side of her face. "Why won't you talk to me? It's not good to keep it in."

He gave her a sad smile. "What is there to say? They took Ethan, they killed Mom. Parris is probably dead. Smithson, too. And we have one lead. A pair of boots."

She set the ice on the bathroom sink and walked over to him. "This isn't your fault."

"They committed the murders, but I didn't stop them," Blake said softly. He let his hands drift over her soft curls. Why wasn't she railing against him, blaming him for her son? Why was she cuddled against him? It didn't make sense.

A sharp knock pounded on the door. Blake tensed. He pushed Amanda into the bathroom. A pause, then two more knocks.

He relaxed a bit. "It's Rafe."

The ex-Green Beret could take her to safety. Blake would take the ransom call. Then he would finish this.

With his Glock in one hand, Blake cracked open the door. The man outside nodded slightly, his visible eye studying Blake with a practiced gaze.

"Blake Redmond?"

He opened the door and let the other man in. Rafe hauled in a heavy duffel, scanned the room, then stared at Amanda. "Safest place," he said. "In the bathroom."

"I want you to take her out of here, Rafe. Find a place to hide her."

"No!" Amanda ran to Blake. "I'm not hiding while Ethan is in danger."

Blake grabbed her. "I need you safe."

"Logan ordered me to back you up," Rafe said. "There's at least three of them from what we can tell. Maybe more. You took out two in the chopper. Going in alone is suicide."

"Gee, thanks, Rafe."

The man smiled. "You're welcome. Besides, I brought a computer and secure internet access. Zane locked it down tight. They can't track it. Your lady can check out the emails. Maybe unlock that file."

Blake didn't have much confidence she'd break the code. They needed Ethan for that. Vince knew what he'd done with the file. He didn't leave a message. Ethan was the key.

Blake forced a look of confidence. "Things are looking up."

A slight hope entered her eyes. He met Rafe's gaze. The man understood the truth. But at least the computer would keep Amanda occupied. And maybe they'd get lucky.

"Set it up," Blake ordered Rafe.

He heaved the duffel onto the bed and unzipped the bag. Blake glanced in and a deadly smile settled in the cold anger of his eyes. "Thank God for firepower."

"That's not the good stuff," Rafe muttered as he took out the laptop. He pulled out several other electronic devices, too. One he attached to the phone. "This will record any conversations and give us the number and location of the originating call. As long as they're not bouncing signals everywhere."

"It's so small," Amanda said.

Rafe handed her the machine and hot spot. "Have at it."

Blake kept glancing back at her while he and Rafe organized the weapons.

"How's your focus?" Rafe asked softly.

Blake pulled a box of ammo for his Glock and set it aside. "I'm fine."

"I could take lead," Rafe commented. "Logan told me about your mother."

"Would *you* let someone else take charge?"

"Point."

It didn't take long to organize the ammunition and equipment.

Rafe settled down in the corner next to Leo and ruffled the dog's ears. "Once we know the plan, I'll find a way to get him to a vet." The dog licked Rafe's hand. "He's a good one."

"Don't think about it," Blake said. "He belongs to Ethan."

Amanda's fingers stilled on the keyboard. Blake touched her shoulder and squeezed lightly. She gave him a shallow smile.

Blake didn't know how long he'd paced when the phone on the bed rang. Amanda looked at it and stilled. She walked over to the bed, her body curved into Blake's.

He picked up the phone. "Redmond."

"We have the boy. Bring the evidence and he lives. Play games with us, he dies."

"How do I know he's okay?" Blake said.

"You don't." The man laughed. "You'll hear from us." He hung up the phone.

"Proof of life?" Rafe said as he fiddled with the recorder.

Blake shook his head.

"Damn." Rafe turned a few knobs. "Not long enough." He glanced at Amanda. "I'm sorry."

Amanda sank to her knees. "I couldn't find anything in the emails. They're just jokes and chitchat. What are we going to do?"

Blake wrapped his arms around her to prop her up. "We'll find him." He glanced at Rafe. "We need a way to open that file."

"I'll call Zane. Maybe he's figured something out."

Rafe dialed the computer expert and Blake pulled Amanda aside. "This is good. They'll call back with a location. A meet. We have more than we had before."

Her distressed expression nearly drained his heart. He could see her desperation to believe, and the fear to allow herself to hope.

Rafe turned and laid the phone on the bed.

"I'm here, Rafe," Zane's gruff voice sounded through the phone.

"They have the boy. They want the evidence. We're out of time."

The man cursed. "I'm no closer. If I had a week… maybe."

"Can you tell how many letters or numbers?" Blake asked.

The sound of clicking keys funneled through the phone. They waited.

Blake gripped Amanda's hand. "Well?"

Zane bit out another curse. "Could be four. Could be twenty-four. I can't tell."

Amanda sank to the floor against the wall, her forehead resting against her knees. He could see the last bit of optimism seeping out of her. "That's it, then," she muttered. "There's not a chance we'll figure out that password."

"She's right," Rafe said quietly. "Even Zane thinks so."

Another loud curse sounded through the phone. Rafe picked up the receiver. "Call us when you have something."

Blake twisted his ball cap around. He looked at Rafe, then Amanda. "Okay, we work with what we have. They want evidence, we'll take them evidence."

"What are you talking about?" Amanda stared at him as if he'd gone mad.

Rafe grinned. "I like the way you think, brother."

AMANDA WALKED BY the phone and glared at it. She couldn't stand the waiting. She glanced at Blake. He'd slipped a knife into his boot and practiced again and again pulling the weapon out with ease.

Most would think he was calm and all business. Not Amanda. She recognized the small tick in his jaw. A small shiver of unease skittered down her spine. He'd been quiet. Too quiet. Not that Blake was overly talkative, but there was a tension in him that made her nervous.

A sharp knock prevented her from trying to reach out once more to the man she'd come to care for. No. Those words were too small for her feelings. She didn't want to say, much less think, the word though. Too many uncertainties.

Blake palmed his Glock and peered through the peephole, then opened the door. Rafe walked in with a sack from an office supply store.

"Did you find a vet?"

"Leo will be fine. Doc is setting his leg. Doesn't look like internal injuries. He'll be playing with Ethan in no time."

Rafe pulled out a folder of printed material, graph

paper, pencils, pens, markers, file folders and a thumb drive and scattered them on the bed. "Logan sent us the Morelli case. We can dupe the evidence. They were into guns, money laundering, you name it. Not unlike our Austin cops."

Amanda poked at the papers. "Will it fool them?"

"Not for long." Blake ripped open the paper. "But we only need a few minutes. Once Rafe's in position, we take out the kidnappers and grab Ethan."

"It's so risky," Amanda said, leafing through the graph paper.

"Rafe and I were trained for this. And it's our only option unless you've remembered anything Ethan said that would help us with the password."

She shook her head in frustration. "What can I do to help?"

Blake passed her a handwritten spreadsheet. "Recreate this. It's evidence from a money-laundering case. Substitute random words for the names to keep it confusing. I'll package everything I can."

Amanda took the papers and a pencil and settled on the bed to copy the lines of numbers.

"I hope the head honcho is in town," Rafe said. "I'd like a shot at him."

"Not before me," Blake said, his voice cold. "Even if he's not here, when we bring Ethan back to Amanda, he might be able to identify enough cops we can get someone to turn."

Her pencil stilled. She couldn't have heard them right. She shot to her feet. "Are you crazy? You are *not* leaving me here."

"It's too dangerous," Blake said, his voice low and urgent.

She glanced over at Rafe, who muttered to himself

as he organized supplies. She took Blake's hand. "He's my son. I'm going with you."

"You'll get in the way. If I have to worry about you, I can't concentrate on protecting Ethan." He put his hands on her shoulders. "I can't risk being distracted."

"What if something happens? There's only two of you."

"Rafe and I can handle it. One of us will bring Ethan back to you. I promise."

She leaned her forehead against him. "I have a bad feeling about this. We don't know how many there are. They're ruthless. I can cover you, Blake. Give me a gun. I know how to use it."

The hotel phone rang.

Rafe stilled and flipped a switch on the electronics. He nodded to Blake.

"Redmond."

"Let me talk to the woman."

Blake motioned to Amanda. *Try to keep them talking,* he mouthed and placed an earpiece in his ear.

"H-hello."

"You have the evidence?" The man's voice was husky with a hint of a Southern drawl.

"Y-yes."

"Where did you find it?"

"I got an email from Vince. There was a link to a file."

A low curse sounded from the phone. "Always was a geek," the man muttered. "Bring me the file. I want a hard copy, all electronic copies and the location of the file. Don't try anything funny, or your son dies."

Blake grabbed the phone. "Where do you want me to meet you?"

"Not you, Redmond. Hawthorne's sister. Only her.

You bring backup, the boy dies. You call in the Feds, the boy dies."

"You don't need her. I'll come alone."

"She won't be able to lie to me." He paused. "And Redmond, we're watching you. We know you've got help in there. If you want to see the kid alive, you'll follow my instructions to the letter. I want to see Amanda Hawthorne at the corner of Main and Third in one hour. She comes alone."

The phone clicked off.

Blake slammed the receiver into the cradle.

"I can't wait to get hold of this guy." Rafe's expression was dark, the patch over his eye making him scary. "They know I'm here. We've lost the element of surprise."

Amanda walked between the two men. "He's my son. I can do this."

Blake sighed and lifted her chin. "You're the bravest woman I know, but—"

"No." She pushed at him. "I can *do* this. For Ethan."

A knock sounded at the hotel room door.

Blake eased toward it gun drawn. Rafe followed. With a quick nod at Amanda, she eased into the entryway of the bathroom. On signal, Blake threw open the door.

A man stood in the doorway hands in the air, palms outstretched.

"Johnson?"

At Blake's incredulous voice, Amanda studied the man's face. He looked like a cop. Definitely.

"Don't shoot," Johnson said.

In one sharp move, Blake pinned the man to the open door. He patted him down and removed a knife and gun, handing them to Rafe.

"Blake, I'm here to help."

He spun Johnson around. "How did you know we were here?"

Amanda squinted at the intruder's face, then her gaze raked up and down his clothes. She'd seen them before. The four-leaf clover patch on his sweater's elbow locked her gaze. It was him. It had to be. "Where's my son?" she screamed. "Where's Ethan?" She hurled herself toward him, but Blake held her back with one arm. She strained against his grip. "He took Ethan away."

Johnson looked right, then left. "I don't have much time. Please, let me in. If only because we were undercover partners. You trusted me once."

"Obviously a mistake."

"I can help you get her son back."

"You have one minute." Blake stepped aside, his Glock pointing at the man's head. "Kidnapping a kid, Johnson? That's lower than the scum you used to arrest."

The detective looked at Amanda. "I'm sorry. I don't know how this happened."

"Sorry doesn't bring my son home to me." Amanda crossed her arms, glaring at him.

The detective flushed, guilt staining his cheeks. "Look, the boss is very, very good at drawing you in. At first you think you're helping get the bad guys who get away with it." He shook his head. "Before you know it, you've crossed a line and he has you."

Amanda gave a snort of disgust. "Coward."

"How many are involved?" Blake asked, giving her a warning look.

"I don't know totals. Farraday and I led the...enforcement team."

"Farraday? From Homicide?" Blake shoved his hand

in his hair. "Bad temper. And always a few tacos short of a combo."

"He's dead," Johnson said. "Boss killed him."

"Is that why you're here?"

Johnson stilled. "Look, I know I screwed up, but this thing has gone way too wrong. My family's at risk, too." He turned to Amanda. "Do you want to save your son's life?"

"What kind of question is that? I'd do anything."

"If you let these guys call the shots, you're all dead. But there might be a way to get out of this thing alive. Interested?"

"I'm listening," Blake said, his voice still suspicious.

"I leave here with Amanda. We go to that abandoned warehouse off Ninth Street. I tell him that she doesn't trust you anymore and went to the drop zone early with the evidence, so I snagged her. She gives my boss the evidence, and you surprise them."

"No way in hell!"

Amanda gripped Blake's arm and studied Johnson. "Why would you take Ethan earlier and help us now?"

"Boss has gone too far." Johnson stared at her, his eyes haunted. "I don't kill kids."

Amanda took in a deep breath. She looked at Blake, the man who had sacrificed everything for her and Ethan. Her heart pounded. She glanced at Rafe, who still had his weapon pointed at Johnson. "I'm going with him."

"I can't let you," Blake said, although he stood, his eyes blazing with golden fire. "I won't."

"We don't have time for a debate. If they discover I'm here, I'm dead." Johnson turned, keeping his hands visible and looking nervously at Rafe's gun. "Don't go trigger-happy. I'm taking something out of my pocket."

"Careful," Blake warned.

"Too late," Johnson said. "Take your chances with my plan, or die in the warehouse after the boss has some fun torturing you and God knows what else. He's gone crazy. He thinks he's above everyone and everything."

Johnson pulled a zip tie from his pocket and faced Amanda. "If you want a chance to save your son, give me your wrists."

"It's too risky," Blake protested.

"If it will save Ethan, I have to take that risk." She cupped his face. "I know what will happen the moment he gets the evidence. At least this way, we have a chance."

Amanda sidestepped Blake and walked to Johnson, hands in front of her. "Do it," she said.

Chapter Thirteen

Blake stared at Amanda's stiff spine, her wrists waiting to be bound. How could things have reached this point? All he'd ever wanted to do was protect her.

Rafe put his hand on Blake's shoulder. "It's our best option. You know that."

"It's not right. I'm putting her in the hands of a killer." He clutched Johnson's collar. "How do I know you're on the level?"

"If we don't follow my plan, you all end up at the warehouse in handcuffs. There are too many men. You won't survive."

"Blake, please, let me go with him."

Amanda turned to Blake, her face pale as the ice that had brought her into his life. He couldn't allow this. There had to be another way.

"I know what you're thinking," she whispered. She framed his face with her hands. "Let me protect my son. You'll get there in time. You *will* save me. I know you will."

Johnson turned to him. "I'll do everything I can to keep them safe."

Blake covered her small hands with his and gripped them tight. He let out a stream of air and hugged her close. "Listen to me. You be smart. You stay alive, however you have to. I'll be there, Amanda. I'll save you and Ethan. I promise."

She smiled at him, her lips trembling. "I know that, Blake. I've always known." She held him close, and her warm breath bathed his ear. "Just like I've always loved you."

His soul split into two. He gripped her tight for one second, then released her. She turned and lifted her arms to Johnson. "I'm ready."

He snapped on the zip ties. "Where's the evidence?"

He held out his hand, and Blake handed over the fake documents, then tucked a thumb drive into Amanda's pocket.

As Johnson escorted her out the door, she looked back at him and smiled, the faith in her eyes nearly knocking him over with its strength. How could she do that?

Blake clutched his Glock as his entire body went alert. She was everything he'd ever wanted.

And he'd let her walk away. Alone.

Not for long. Blake grabbed extra ammo and tucked a knife into his boot. "We have surprise on our side. Amanda will do her part. Now we've got to do ours."

JOHNSON GRIPPED HER TIGHT as he led her into an abandoned warehouse. A man waited across the room, his demeanor calm and satisfied, spinning the revolving chamber of an old handgun. The Colt that belonged to Blake's granddad. He looked vaguely familiar, but she couldn't place him.

She didn't think he'd been to Vince's house, so where had she seen the man's face? Television, newspaper?

He crossed the room to Johnson. "Did you get the evidence?"

Amanda's hands shook as Johnson passed over the fake evidence and the thumb drive.

His boss paused. "Where's Blake?"

"I had to kill him," Johnson said, his gaze down low. "I'm sorry. He came at me. I had no choice."

The man's face flushed. "You'd better hope I get the right answers from this file, Johnson. It might put me in a mood where that's not your third strike."

Johnson swallowed and nodded as he shifted closer to Amanda.

"Are these the only copies?" Johnson's boss gripped Amanda's face and stared into her eyes. Terrified, she looked at the man who'd killed Vince, who'd murdered Blake's family.

A thin smile creased his clean-shaven face. "Scared of me, are you? No need. I get what I want, you go free."

She didn't believe him. He had cold eyes. He wouldn't let them go. And when he found out the files were fake… She had to stall for time. Blake was coming. He'd be here soon.

"I want to see Ethan," she said, channeling the courage the man she loved would have shown in the same situation.

"Yancy, get out here!" Another man walked into the room with a laptop. The boss handed him the *evidence*. "Check it out. Find out who the traitor is."

"You have the file," Amanda said. "Where's my son?"

"Standing up to me." He ran his hand down her cheek. "Something your brother didn't have the courage to do. He cowered. I could've used someone like you in my organization."

Amanda shivered in disgust, but didn't shrink away

from him…or run. Blake had taught her to face her fears. Hiding was no solution. "My son."

"I like your guts," he said, a tinge of regret in his voice. He walked across the room and opened a door. Ethan sat bound to a chair, cringing away from the door.

He was alive.

Her entire body trembled with relief, and her son's terror-filled gaze fueled her courage. This man would pay for what he'd done to Ethan.

Then he saw her. "Mommy!"

He squirmed against his bindings.

"Please," she begged.

"She might be able to control him, sir," Johnson said.

His boss's lip curled up. "Cut the ties. I can afford to be generous."

Amanda ran over to Ethan. With a glare, she untied the ropes around her son and pulled him tight to her. That they let her hold him, scared her to death. She must stall for Blake's arrival.

She rocked Ethan back and forth, reveling in the warmth of his alive body. "I'm so glad you're okay."

"Mommy!" Ethan hugged her neck and pointed his finger at the man standing in front of her and whispered in her ear. "He has the dragons. He hurt Uncle Vince."

Their captor looked down at his boots. His eyes hardened. "So you did see me. Not that it changes anything."

"Please just let us disappear," Amanda begged. "I promise we'll vanish. We won't say anything. I don't even know who you are."

"Hey, Boss," Yancy said. "We got a problem. The evidence is fake."

DAMN.

Blake watched the plan's implosion from a small gap

in the warehouse's steel walls. "Their computer guy is good."

Lieutenant Paul Irving from Internal Affairs rounded on Amanda. He raised the Colt .45. "I don't play games." He turned the weapon on Ethan. "I warned you."

Blake raced around the warehouse followed closely by Rafe. He burst through the door. "Stop. I know where the real file is."

Several men followed Blake in.

"Cover them," Irving said, his smile slow. He turned on Johnson. He raised his weapon and pointed it at the cop's head. "You just sacrificed your family for the Hawthorne kid."

Johnson's face lost what little color it had.

Irving pulled the trigger and Johnson's body fell to the floor.

"One piece of business completed. Now on to the next." He propped his boot on a stool, the fire coming out of the red dragon's mouth visible from beneath his black jeans. He stared down Blake. "You've been trouble since you made detective. Do you even know how easy it was to get rid of you?"

"My family's accident."

Irving shrugged. "It was a start, but I needed more. Farraday got the idea. A few fireworks can make a horse a deadly weapon."

Blake's jaw tightened as the realization shot through him. His father, Smithson. He pushed back the fury. He'd grieve later. "You have us, but I can offer you something in return for letting Amanda and Ethan run. I can show you the real file. Just let me at the computer."

Blake started across the room.

"No." Irving raised his hand, and Blake paused in stride. "I want the woman at the keyboard. Alone."

Amanda shook her head. "I'm not leaving my son. Not ever again."

Irving grabbed her by the arm and dragged her to the chair, but she didn't let go of Ethan's hand. Blake cursed under his breath.

"Sit down. Keep the kid quiet."

"Go to your email, Amanda," Blake said sharply, hoping the tactic would work.

She looked down at the computer, then glared at him. "I can't believe you're doing this. You betrayed me. And Ethan. You're no better than him." She nodded at Irving. "A murderer." She gave him a look of hatred, her hands planted on her hips.

Good girl. Every second counted.

"Enough of your histrionics!" Irving said. "Show me the file."

Amanda opened the browser, then stared up at him. "How do I know you'll let us go?"

"If you don't show me that file, your boy dies. Now." Irving grabbed Ethan and held him by the neck.

Damn it. If only Amanda hadn't taken Ethan over there. It would make Blake's job that much harder.

"Please don't hold him so tight."

Irving gripped Ethan even tighter. Blake struggled not to go after the bastard. He sent up a prayer. Patience. The timing had to be perfect.

Amanda played the game well. She had grit, but he could see Irving losing his temper. She stalled as long as she could. But she recognized the danger, because after a few seconds Amanda logged into her email. "It's at this link."

"Click to open it."

The password dialogue box popped up.

"We don't know the password," Blake said.

Irving let out a string of curses. Ethan whimpered in his arms.

"Leave him alone." Amanda stood up and took a step to Irving.

"I want the evidence. I want to know who betrayed me. Vince couldn't have had enough information to tie me to everything."

No wonder. Everything made sense now.

"You really should've been smarter," Blake taunted. "You killed Vince before he could let anyone in on the password. We have two chances or the file will be destroyed."

"Mommy! Mommy! He's hurting me." Ethan squirmed and kicked out against Irving.

Irving spun Ethan toward him. "You saw me shoot your uncle."

Ethan's face was full of terror.

"No!" Amanda screamed.

Blake wanted to rip the guy's arm off, but there were too many guns pointed at Amanda and Ethan.

"I'll do the same to your mom right now if you don't tell me the password."

Ethan's eyes widened, and he started crying.

"The kid is five," Blake snapped. "He doesn't know what a password is."

"You get him to tell me, or I kill you one at a time. Starting with *her*."

Relieved at the excuse to get closer to Ethan, Blake nodded and walked across to them. He'd be close enough to shield them with his body if bullets started flying.

He knelt in front of Ethan. The boy trembled and his eyes were glazed over. "It's okay, Ethan. It'll be okay. What did Vince say to you before he died?"

Ethan looked at his mother, then at Blake.

"Do you trust me, Ethan?" Blake asked softly.

"Joey's in the clouds," the boy muttered.

"Who's Joey?" Irving snapped.

"Don't you remember? He was my son. You murdered him."

At those words, at least a dozen men streamed into the warehouse. Blake clutched Ethan in one arm and bounded toward Amanda, knocking her from the chair protecting them with his body. The table clattered and the Colt .45 tumbled to the floor.

Shots rang out in the small warehouse. Ethan and Amanda huddled beneath him. Blake raised his head scanning the room, his entire body tense. He reached for the Colt.

A flash of heat scorched his shoulder, but he ignored the pain. At least his arm hadn't gone numb. Making sure Ethan and Amanda weren't in a line of sight, he gripped the butt of the gun.

Irving cursed and dived toward them, gun drawn.

Blake raised his granddad's Colt. He took aim at the traitor's eyes and pulled the trigger.

THE WAREHOUSE SWARMED with men. Amanda stared at what was left of Irving—the evil man responsible for so many deaths. His brains spilled onto the concrete floor. She shifted Ethan's face away from the gore. Irving had deserved the undignified death.

Blake's weight rested on top of her, warm and comforting and very heavy. "Is it safe?" she asked.

"Maybe," Blake said.

She pushed at his shoulder a bit, and he groaned, shifting off her.

"What's wrong?"

"Nothing."

Ethan whimpered and stuck his hand up to her face. "Blood, Mommy."

She gasped. "We need a doctor!"

"Not me, Mommy," Ethan said, tears streaming down his face. "Sheriff Blake. He got shot like Uncle Vince."

Blood seeped through Blake's shirt, and her heart sank. She reached out a shaking hand. "What did you do, Blake Redmond?"

He shrugged and couldn't hide the wince, but that didn't stop him from tugging Ethan onto his lap. "I'm not going to die, son. It's just a scratch." He brushed back the boy's hair. "Are you okay? Did they hurt you?"

Ethan shoved up his sleeve. "I fell down. I got a scratch, too."

Blake made a show of checking out Ethan's skinned elbow.

A paramedic ran to them, took one look at Blake's shoulder and kneeled down. "The boy comes first," Blake said, his face harsh.

The EMT didn't argue. Amanda wouldn't have, either. The man certainly got what he wanted when he turned into the great stone face. After checking out Ethan, the paramedic pulled out a pair of scissors and turned to Blake. "You're still bleeding," the man muttered. "You need stitches."

"Later. I have some business to take care of."

Amanda hovered near Blake, holding Ethan in her lap. Even though he squirmed, he didn't want to leave her side. She didn't intend to let him out of her sight for a very long time.

Irving's body had been carted off, and several others were led away. Half the men were in uniforms and the other half weren't.

"Can we trust them?" she whispered to Blake.

"No," he said. "A lot of answers died with Irving."

His face intent, he studied the room even as he held her hand, his thumb caressing her palm.

"Are we still in danger?" She clutched his hand and pulled Ethan closer.

Blake tugged the knife from his boot. "I'm not taking chances. Rafe's covering us."

She turned her head, and noticed the man, silent, holding his weapon at the ready.

Ethan looked up at Blake in awe. "You made the bad man with the boots go away," he said. "Uncle Vince said you would."

Blake ruffled his hair. "You were very brave, Ethan. I'm proud of you."

Ethan's chest puffed out, and Amanda's heart warmed, even as uncertainty shifted through her. What would happen now?

How long would they have to be on guard? Would Blake want to be a part of their lives when her family— her, Ethan and Vince—had cost Blake his family?

She rubbed her eyes. She loved Blake. As she watched him with Ethan, she recognized she'd never felt this kind of trust. Before, she'd never felt certain of anyone or anything. But she could count on Blake. Through the best and the worst. Through anything.

Ethan tugged on Blake's shirt. "Are we going to stay with you?" he asked.

Blake stilled and his face took on a cautious expression. "I think I'd like that, Ethan." He glanced at Amanda. "I guess it's up to your mother."

A skip of hope flittered through Amanda, its shimmer of warmth reawakening the optimism she'd buried for so long.

"Did you bring my truck?" Ethan asked. "Do you think Joey would mind if I kept his?"

A wave of hurt dimmed Blake's eyes, but he smiled at Ethan. "Your truck is safe. And I think Joey would like you to have it." Blake looked at Amanda. "Joey. Joey's in the clouds. What was it Zane said about the cloud?"

Amanda bowed her head and ran through the conversation in her mind. "That Vince had stashed the file in the cloud somewhere."

"Joey's in the clouds."

A cop had grabbed the laptop, and Blake raced over, despite his injury, and took it from the uniform.

He protested, "It's evidence."

"I might have more," Blake said. "Just give me a minute."

Blake didn't have to reboot. The machine had gone to sleep. The pop-up warning came up. Blake typed in J-O-E-Y.

The hard drive whirred.

The file opened.

"Vince, you son of a gun!"

Amanda leaned over Blake's shoulder.

Blake. Buddy, if you're reading this, I've screwed up and died on you. Man, I'm sorry I couldn't tell you I was undercover. I know you thought I'd turned. I hate that.

I was under orders, and I thought I was protecting you by not telling you and getting you out of town. I'm more sorry than I could ever express that I couldn't save Joey or Kathy. The bastards killed your dad, too. The head honcho is losing it. I knew it wouldn't be long before they went after your mom. Watch out for her.

I'm begging you. Please protect Ethan and Amanda, too. The kingpin is Lieutenant Irving, but until recently, everything was circumstantial. Not anymore. He's making mistakes. I've zipped up bank statements and a money trail. I've also included a list of all the officers involved. It'll make you sick. I have an informant inside his organization: Marquez. Contact him if you can. He will help. Make sure he gets a break.

Tell Amanda and Ethan I loved them. And I always will.
Your best friend. Always.
Vince

Amanda lowered her head. Her eyes burned at the truth. She'd doubted Vince, and she hated herself for that.

Blake cleared his throat and clicked on one of the files. He scanned the men being worked on by the emergency crews while under guard. "Marquez?" he called out.

The man who'd held the gun to Blake's back lifted his head. "What's it to you?"

"Take the cuffs off Marquez," Blake said.

Shaun O'Connor hurried over. "What are you doing?"

"We found the evidence."

Blake shifted back and let him take a look at the list of names. His eyes darkened in anger. With a nod, he whispered to one of the men near him.

Suddenly, two cops were handcuffed and led away. "I can't believe some of these guys. I trusted them," O'Connor said.

Blake turned to Amanda. "You're safe now." He

twirled his finger through her hair. "You were right all along. Vince was a hero."

Amanda looked up at the golden fire in his eyes. "Blake, I—"

He touched his finger to her lips. "Don't. We've been through a lot in the past few days," he said softly. "I know you said some things to me in the motel room. The feelings might not be real."

"But—"

He pulled her to him, and his body trembled against hers. "I want to earn those words, Amanda. Even if you don't feel them now, I want you to stay. I want to earn your love. I want what my folks had."

The underlying sadness in his voice broke her heart. She hugged him tight. "You don't have to earn anything, Blake. I love you. I was attracted to you from the day I met you. I wanted you from that first Christmas kiss." She cupped his face. "But you've shown me a lifetime of love over the last few days. You know what's important in life. But I need to know how *you* feel. You've never told me."

Blake swooped down and took her mouth with his, the intensity in his kiss screaming his feelings. He raised his head. "I love you, Amanda. With all my heart. I'll protect you and our family with every ounce of strength I have. I'll cherish you for as long as we live. If you'll let me."

A round of applause sounded around them. Rafe tipped his hat and walked out of the warehouse as if he were never there.

Amanda's cheeks heated. Blake pulled her into his arms and hugged her tight. "Let's make a family, Amanda. You and me and Ethan."

"I can't say yes," she said softly.

He pulled away from her slack-jawed, and his face turned cautious. "What are you saying?"

"We have to ask Ethan."

Blake knelt down in front of her son. "What do you think, buddy?"

"Are you going to be my daddy?" he asked.

"If you'll let me, I want you to come live with me."

Ethan tilted his head, as if considering a huge problem. "Can I ride the tractor?"

"No!" Amanda said.

"You bet," Blake said at the same time.

"Blake—"

"With supervision."

"Can Leo be my dog?"

"Sure thing," Blake said. "I think he picked you already."

"Then it's okay." He looked up at them. "Can we go home? I want to play with Leo."

Amanda smiled and folded her fingers into Blake's. "I thought fairy tales were for little girls, but you changed my mind, Blake Redmond. I've found my happily ever after."

Epilogue

"Blake Redmond!"

Amanda stood on the porch and stared at Ethan as he waved at her from atop the tractor, Leo running at his side. That dog was never two feet from her son.

"We agreed not until he's ten!" Amanda glared at her husband.

Blake grinned at her, that familiar mischievous glint of gold in his eyes. "He's a boy. He needs to stretch his wings."

She waddled out to him, her hand on her swollen belly. "You are *not* making your wife or our child happy."

Blake stroked her belly, and the baby kicked against her side. She winced a bit at their active child and sent a worried glance toward Ethan. He shouldn't be driving that thing.

Her husband slipped around her and wrapped her in his arms, pressing in close. She rested against the hard planes of his body and sighed as his lips nipped her ear. "Parris is walking right beside him," he said quietly. "They're hardly moving."

She turned in his arms and glared at him, her belly poking at him. "You did that just to get a rise out of me."

He kissed her nose. "Maybe."

"Now, none of that. That's how you two got in this

predicament." Nancy Redmond's voice filtered out from the screen door, a wide smile on her face, and a brand-new gold band shining on her left hand.

Amanda sighed as Blake hugged his mother, his eyes closed tight. She knew every time he saw her he flashed back to those few days he'd believed he'd lost her.

To try to avoid the Austin police, Nancy and Parris had ended up stranded in his fishing cabin for several days, with no cell service and no way to communicate. When they'd finally made contact, it was the first time Amanda had seen her husband cry. The second was when she'd told him she was pregnant.

They'd been through so much. Everyone had. The blows kept coming. It hadn't taken long to realize Donna, the department dispatcher, had been killed in Nancy's house. Irving's greed had destroyed too many lives. But life did go on. And now, almost a year later, life was very, very good. She'd found the best man and best father a woman could ask for—if a bit bossy at times. Still, she had complete confidence he would fight for her and cherish her and their children. And if she occasionally had to take him down a peg or two…she touched her abdomen. Makeup sessions could be more than wonderful.

Blake hugged Amanda to him. She nestled close and gazed at the blue and pink clouds billowing on the horizon. Sugar stood in his pen, calm and serene, as if he, too, knew the murderers had paid and that healing had taken root for his family.

Blake kissed her temple. "Are we still happily ever after?"

She wrapped her arms around his neck. "More than ever."

* * * * *

COMING NEXT MONTH from Harlequin® Intrigue®
AVAILABLE AUGUST 7, 2012

#1365 GAGE
The Lawmen of Silver Creek Ranch
Delores Fossen
After faking his death to protect his family, CIA agent Gage Ryland is forced to secretly return from the grave to save his ex, Lynette Herrington, who's carrying a secret of her own.

#1366 SECRET ASSIGNMENT
Cooper Security
Paula Graves
On a visit to a private island, an archivist stumbles onto an invasion, forcing her to work with the handsome caretaker to learn who will stop at nothing to gain access to the island—and why.

#1367 KANSAS CITY COWBOY
The Precinct: Task Force
Julie Miller
Sheriff Boone Harrison and police psychologist Kate Kilpatrick couldn't be more different. But trusting each other is the only way to catch a killer...and find a second chance at love.

#1368 MOMMY MIDWIFE
Cassie Miles
Nine months after a night she'll never forget, a pregnant midwife must trust the baby's father, a man she barely knows, to rescue her from the madman who wants her baby.

#1369 COPY THAT
HelenKay Dimon
A girl-next-door gets sucked into a dangerous new life when a wounded border patrol agent lands on her doorstep, with gunmen hot on his trail.

#1370 HER COWBOY AVENGER
Thriller
Kerry Connor
Her husband's murder turned her into an outcast and a suspect—and the only man who can help her is the tall, dark cowboy she thought she'd never see again.

You can find more information on upcoming Harlequin® titles, free excerpts and more at www.Harlequin.com.

HICNM0712

REQUEST YOUR FREE BOOKS!
2 FREE NOVELS PLUS 2 FREE GIFTS!

Harlequin

INTRIGUE

BREATHTAKING ROMANTIC SUSPENSE

Werewolf and elite U.S. Navy SEAL, Matt Parker, must set aside his prejudices and partner with beautiful Fae Sienna McClare to find a magic orb that threatens to expose the secret nature of his entire team.

Harlequin® Nocturne presents the debut of beloved author Bonnie Vanak's new miniseries, PHOENIX FORCE.

Enjoy a sneak preview of THE COVERT WOLF, available August 2012 from Harlequin® Nocturne.

Sienna McClare was Fae, accustomed to open air and fields. Not this boxy subway car.

As the oily smell of fear clogged her nostrils, she inhaled deeply, tried thinking of tall pines waving in the wind, the chatter of birds and a deer cropping grass. A wolf watching a deer, waiting. Prey. Images of fangs flashing, tearing, wet sounds…

No!

She fought the panic freezing her blood. And was gradually able to push the fear down into a dark spot deep inside her. The stench of Draicon werewolf clung to her like cheap perfume.

Sienna hated glamouring herself as a Draicon werewolf, but it was necessary if she was going to find the Orb of Light. Someone had stolen the Orb from her colony, the Los Lobos Fae. A Draicon who'd previously been seen in the area was suspected. Sienna had eagerly seized the chance to help when asked because finding it meant she would no longer be an outcast. The Fae had cast her out when she turned twenty-one because she was the bastard child of a sweet-faced Fae and a Draicon killer. But if she found the Orb, Sienna could return to the only home she'd known. It also meant she could recover her lost memories.

Every time she tried searching for her past, she met with a closed door. Who was she? Which side ruled her?

Fae or Draicon?

Draicon, no way in hell.

Sensing someone staring, she glanced up, saw a man across the aisle. He was heavily muscled and radiated power and confidence. Yet he also had the face of a gentle warrior. Sienna's breath caught. She felt a stir of sexual chemistry.

He was as lonely and grief stricken as she was. Her heart twisted. Who had hurt this man? She wanted to go to him, comfort him and ease his sorrow. Sienna smiled.

An odd connection flared between them. Sienna locked her gaze to his, desperately needing someone who understood.

Then her nostrils flared as she caught his scent. Hatred boiled to the surface. Not a man. Draicon.

The enemy.

Find out what happens next in THE COVERT WOLF by Bonnie Vanak.

Available August 2012 from Harlequin® Nocturne wherever books are sold.